WORKS BY
GEOFFREY DOUGLAS

Class: The Wreckage of an American Family

Dead Opposite: The Lives and Loss of Two American Boys

The Game of Their Lives

The Classmates: Privilege, Chaos, and the End of an Era

The Grifter, the Poet, and the Runaway Train

PRAISE FOR
GEOFFREY DOUGLAS

For *Class: The Wreckage of an American Family*

"Mr. Douglas reconstructs a devastating portrait of the parents he hardly knew . . . a fascinating and perceptive piece of social history."

—*Wall Street Journal*

"A ruthlessly candid history . . . a significant sociological study as well as a wrenching memoir of great poignancy."

—*Publishers Weekly*

"The ghost of F. Scott Fitzgerald haunts the corridors of Geoffrey Douglas's pain-soaked but splendidly constructed prose. But this memoir's moral accomplishment surpasses even its literary grace . . . an act of heroic redemption."

—Ron Powers, author, *Flags of Our Fathers*, and winner of the Pulitzer Prize for Criticism

"A sad, intense memoir . . . a cautionary tale about what happens when privilege deteriorates into mere carelessness and self-indulgence."

—*The Washington Post*

For *Dead Opposite: The Lives and Loss of Two American Boys*

"Douglas's book raises important questions at a time when our bankrupt answer to crime is more prisons."

—*People*

"Douglas has opted not to write the standard 'true crime'
book . . . Instead, [he] attempts something more ambitious—
to find the 'tremendous human commonness' between two
disparate families riven by the same act."

—*Hartford Courant*

"You may find yourself stunned anew by the width of the chasm that
separates this country's haves from its have-nots."

—*The Washington Post Book Review*

"Don't miss this powerful, eloquent and accomplished book."

—*New Haven Advocate*

For *The Game of Their Lives*

"A simple yet compelling account . . . Douglas's writing style reflects
the straight-ahead execution of that 1950 team. The New Hampshire
author isn't flashy, doesn't feint or dodge."

—*Chicago Tribune*

"Douglas excels and becomes almost poetic in his depiction
of life in the ethnic big-city ghettos."

—*Publishers Weekly*

"The evocation of a not-so-distant past of close-knit, vibrant
neighborhoods and ethnic enclaves weaves a spell."

—*NY Daily News*

"Written by critically acclaimed author Geoffrey Douglas, and now a film directed by David Anspaugh (*Hoosiers*), *The Game of Their Lives* takes us back to a time before million-dollar contracts and commercial endorsements, and introduces us to the athletes—the Americans— who showed the world just how far a long shot could really go."

—Barnes & Noble

For *The Classmates*

"Douglas writes in a spare, elegiac style that makes one feel he is sitting at vespers, quietly murmuring the evensong prayer."

—*Newsweek*

"A touching, troubling book that should be read by every commencement speaker before dropping the leaden mantle of expectations on another graduating class."

—*Yankee*

"A book saturated with the emotions unleashed by a group of middle-aged men's miraculous reconnection . . . frequently moving."

—*Kirkus*

"Both a capsule history of an era and a literary tour de force."

—Hachette Books

LOVE
in a
DARK
PLACE

This is a work of fiction. All of the main characters, as well as the story itself, are imaginary. At the same time, the novel's historical setting—including certain named public figures and contemporaneous events—are based on actual persons and happenings of the time, in this case 1980s Atlantic City.

Published by Greenleaf Book Group Press
Austin, Texas
www.gbgpress.com

Distributed by Greenleaf Book Group

For ordering information or special discounts for bulk purchases, please contact Greenleaf Book Group at PO Box 91869, Austin, TX 78709, 512.891.6100.

Design and composition by Greenleaf Book Group and Mimi Bark
Cover design by Greenleaf Book Group and Mimi Bark
Cover image used under license from ©AdobeStock/Christian Hinkle

Publisher's Cataloging-in-Publication data is available.

Print ISBN: 979-8-88645-330-0

eBook ISBN: 979-8-88645-331-7

To offset the number of trees consumed in the printing of our books, Greenleaf donates a portion of the proceeds from each printing to the Arbor Day Foundation. Greenleaf Book Group has replaced over 50,000 trees since 2007.

Printed in the United States of America on acid-free paper

25 26 27 28 29 30 31 32   10 9 8 7 6 5 4 3 2 1

First Edition

LOVE
in a
DARK
PLACE

a novel

GEOFFREY DOUGLAS

GREENLEAF
BOOK GROUP PRESS

One

———

February 2018

Sometime during the night of October 12, 2017, a sixty-one-year-old woman named Sarah Holmes—or Sarah Sullivan or Sarah Michaelis, depending on what records you go by—walked fully clothed into a deep pool of the Shawsheen River in northeast Massachusetts, a mile south of the New Hampshire line, where she drowned. The police report called it an accident, noting that "Deceased's knuckles and fingers were bloodied in a manner consistent with clawing at rocks"—in other words, that she'd tried her best to live. But she went in at a spot where the current was strongest, and it was reported soon after that she'd never learned to swim.

***

Four months later, in mid-February of the following year, Harry Hopper, a professor of English at nearby New Boston College, sits by himself in a faded green parka and woolen ski hat, on the deck of his house at a bend of the river just upstream from where the woman's body was found. The temperature is in the teens, as it has been for weeks now, and the river is mostly frozen, clogged from bank to bank with great, room-size slabs of ice that slog downstream, occasionally bumping, like tired old bears at the zoo. The man has sat here almost every day lately, often for hours, sometimes reading, or trying to—a book, or a student's paper—more often just staring out at the floes, as though they might hold an answer.

When the police had arrived at his door, then sat with him at his kitchen table, he had told them Sarah Holmes was an old friend with health problems and nowhere else to turn, and that he'd been trying to help her through a bad time. All this was true as far as it went, but had led to questions that skirted issues he wasn't anxious to address. A day later, when they'd kept pushing—a local cop and a Boston detective, now at a scarred wooden table in a witness interview room at the local fire station (strangely, much like the room where he'd first met the woman)—he had told them as much as he thought he needed to.

"Does this Sarah have any family?"

"There's a daughter. Near Philadelphia. I have her number if you want."

"Where was Sarah living when she died?"

"At the Ebb Tide Motel, about eight miles up Route 12. Since last June. She was renting by the week. You'll find all her stuff there."

"So she was turning tricks there?"

He pretended to be more surprised by this than he was, though he knew there must have been a background check.

"Turning tricks? No man, she wasn't turning tricks. She was close to sixty years old."

"Sixty-one, actually. And there's a reason for the question—we have her charged with soliciting just last year. In Covington, Kentucky, under a couple of different names."

"I didn't know that."

This was true. He hadn't known any of it—about Kentucky, the recent soliciting, the couple of names. But it didn't surprise him.

"So what was she doing at the motel?"

"I told you—trying to get better, trying to dry out. She was an alcoholic."

"Was she working?"

"She had been, part-time at Costco in the produce section."

"Part-time at Costco. That was paying for the motel?"

"I was helping her."

"Uh-huh. And why were you helping her?"

"I told you already. She was broke, she was trying to quit booze. She needed help."

"How long have you known this person?"

"We met in the eighties. But we'd been out of touch since then. Till last June."

"How would you describe your relationship?"

"I told you. She was a friend."

"Were you intimate?"

"No."

"Not ever?"

"For a little while, a long time ago. Years ago. But not since. As I keep telling you, officer, she was a friend."

He had a sense at first that they didn't believe him, then came to see that they probably did, before concluding near the end that they didn't much care either way. Which was a relief to him—the full truth being too complicated to try to explain, to them or to himself.

***

He has lived the last sixteen years by himself in this same small house in the Merrimack Valley, on the southern bank of the river. It is a region known for its old mills and small colleges, at one of which he teaches: two journalism courses a semester, plus Freshman Comp. He's been tenured for a while now, on the strength of not very much: no advanced degrees, no books published, and fewer years in the news business than he likes to admit. But he gets along with people, won a handful of awards a long time ago and is known to be "passionate" in class. At a college such as New Boston, that can sometimes be enough.

He is sixty-five, tall and not yet gray, with a vestigial handsomeness that passes as distinguished to others but no longer matters to him—a stage of life that comes for some of us, when self-assessment has turned from serious to somber and the future, already narrower than anything we'd scripted or imagined, has ceased to beckon and begun instead to loom. He is not the four- or five-book author he'd pictured at thirty, or the settled husband, or the well-traveled Renaissance man. The bank owns most of the little Cape he lives in, and what he has in savings might not carry him more than a year. He worries sometimes about the prospect of a rocky winding-down.

But most days he is content with life, even happy at times. Or was, before October. The river, the town, the college, the city an hour south of him, the mountains an hour north. He's made several good friends at the college, and one or two more nearby. His students, or most of them, are earnest and hard-trying: "None of the shimmering brilliance you see in Cambridge," he wrote in an email to a colleague not long ago, "but none of the entitlement either. They make you want to do right by them. And most of the time I think we do."

He has a grown son from a long-ago marriage, now the editor of a travel magazine in New York, whom he sees less often than he'd like. And there is a good woman in his life—Julia is her name—a tall, dark-haired sociology professor at UMass in Boston. They met at a time, years before Harry's own professor days, when, adrift, unhappy and drinking too much, he had written a freelance piece for a local magazine about Boston street people. The story had touched her (among her research subjects were homeless and abused women) and she had contacted him. They remained friends for years, then became lovers. For Harry, who by then had given up on love, or passion or intimacy or much of anything beyond sex, their bond renewed his belief in at least one or two of those things. "Life at its best is a continuing miracle," Julia had written in a note she left taped to his bathroom mirror a year or two before. And he's come to believe, over time, that there is truth in this.

Still, though the two of them rarely fight over anything that matters, and talk now and again about a future, she remains in her walk-up on Marlborough Street in Boston and he twenty miles north in his Cape. And if you were to ask him why, he might have trouble answering.

***

He had met Sarah more than thirty years before, in Atlantic City in the summer of 1983, midway through his time as a reporter for the daily there. She was an escort. She called herself Dawn. He didn't ask her real name; it didn't matter for the story he was working on: about the different strata of prostitutes in the resort—the streetwalker, the b-girl, the escort, the private hire—where they came from, the dangers they navigated, the sorts of women they were. Depending on the night and the traffic in town, she was a fit for any of the top three tiers: pretty, clean, under thirty-five, adept enough at small talk, a fitting option for a weekend convention. It was the sort of story *The Herald* in those days—with new casinos sprouting like weeds along the Boardwalk and the city awash in any vice you could name—sent its reporters on every day.

She was in jail when they met, caught up in a sting by an undercover cop. She gave her age as twenty-six, though she could have passed for younger. They had talked for half an hour in an orange-brick visitors' room. He liked her, as much as you can like anyone at a time and place like that. She seemed different from the others: smarter, less angry, better-spoken, less beaten-down. And lovely to look at, truly lovely: slight and pale-skinned, with blue-green eyes that seemed to him somehow sad and dreamily unfocused. Her hair was thick and brown and fell in wavy mats to her shoulders. There was a freshness about her he couldn't quite believe. Although the answers she gave to his questions—Where was she from? Where was she living? Was she working alone or with a pimp?—were as hollow and false as all the rest.

It was more than a year before he saw her again: by accident, on a weeknight in the late summer of '84, sitting at the mezzanine bar just off the casino floor at Trump Plaza, which had opened three months before. He had spent the evening playing blackjack, had won a little money and was in an upbeat mood. He enjoyed the game—it was fast-paced and streaky, and appealed to what he liked to call his left-brained side. Several times in his twenties, he had caught the midnight flight from New York to San Juan ($99 round-trip on the old Eastern Air Lines), where he'd spent the afternoons drinking rum cocktails by the pool and his nights at the blackjack tables. He hadn't played again till recently, after a story he wrote on card counters had rekindled the old spark. He played now sometimes after work, when he could find a low-minimum table.

He recognized her right away: just as fresh, just as pretty. It was clear from the dress she was wearing, a low-cut black number with lavender piping, and from the liquid languor with which she covered her share of the bar, that she was still turning tricks.

He asked if he could join her. She looked at him blankly for a second, as though trying to shake off some reverie he'd intruded on, then raised her eyes and smiled:

"Oh, hi there, Mister Ace Reporter. You looking for another interview with the 'sad-eyed siren'? I liked that, that was pretty good. But not tonight. No questions tonight, okay?"

He promised no questions, and she invited him to sit down. They talked for twenty minutes about not very much before she asked him, almost flatly, as though it were the most natural response in the world to whatever he'd just said, "So you want to take me to bed?"

It was Harry's first time with a prostitute, though he tried not to show it. They were together an hour. She charged him $150, about what he'd won at the tables. He left baffled. For all her put-on hooker's art, she gave her body with a tenderness that seemed almost afraid of itself. And she wore that same sadness. You couldn't miss it, but you couldn't touch it either. It felt just out of reach to him. Everything about her felt just out of reach.

"Are you as sad as you seem?" he asked her at the end. She had collected her money and was standing at the door.

She shook her head, smiled almost sweetly, and said she supposed she was sad sometimes, "like anyone," but that "The next time I see you I'll try to be more jolly."

He ignored the first reference, though it had occurred to him already that he might want to see her again. "I don't need you to be jolly," he said. "I guess I just don't like the idea that you're sad." He thought as soon as he said it what an odd thing that must sound like to her.

"You're a very sweet man," she said. "And I really am a siren, you know."

He asked if she knew what a siren was. "Whatever you *want* it to be," she said. "Whatever makes you crazy." And she gave a quick giggle, poked him once lightly with her index finger in the ribs, and was gone.

***

He remembers that moment often these days. And the memory of it, sitting on his little deck in the freezing winter of his sixty-sixth year, seems to begin in his head and spiral down through his chest and groin like a current. He can still feel it, the poke in his ribs, her teasing voice, the small, delighted quiver it had caused in him at the time.

Two

————

June 2017

She was the last off the bus, leaning on her daughter's arm as she disembarked and made her way in slow, careful steps toward the gate. She was waif-thin, and looked far older than he'd imagined, the pieces of her face loose and fallen in on themselves like soggy dough, her shoulders rounded forward so as to nearly mold with her neck. Yet he knew her instantly, even from twenty feet away through the terminal window's grimy glass. The way she carried herself, under the oversized sweatshirt she wore, for all its unsteadiness, was unmistakable. Her hair, though as lifeless now as combed-out cobwebs, was still more brown than gray, and fell to her shoulders exactly as he remembered. And her eyes, he saw as she drew closer, still held their dreamy sadness.

For Harry, it was like looking at a well-remembered portrait, remastered now so as to somehow leave the essence intact while at the same time perverting the features. He was struck almost dumb by the sudden realness of it all.

"Not the beauty anymore, am I, Harry?"

It was the first thing she said to him. She said it numbly, as though half-asleep, undercut now by her weak attempt at a smile. Her eyes, framed underneath by half-circles that looked almost painted on, seemed focused somewhere over his shoulder. They were standing—Sarah, Harry, and Sarah's timid, blandly pretty daughter, Maryanne, who looked to be about thirty—just inside the gate at the terminal in Boston. The bus had come from Philadelphia, where Sarah had been in some sort of halfway house—Harry had never quite gotten the details. They had two suitcases between them, one small, one large, both badly worn. Harry guessed they'd probably come from a thrift shop.

He hugged her, and could feel her wobble unsurely as she moved against his chest. Her arms were sticks. He couldn't see her legs under the ridiculous, army-surplus trousers she wore, but assumed they must be as well. But the clothes were clean. And she smelled strongly of soap. It was clear she'd made an effort.

"It's wonderful to see you," he said.

It wasn't wonderful, of course. It was heartbreaking, as he'd known it would be. But there was something else too. He was frightened. Instantly, almost reflexively frightened, from the moment he saw her through the terminal window, frightened in a way he couldn't name or understand or even recognize right away for what it was, only as something terribly unsettling. The way a dream can still hold you on waking, even when only the barest sense of it remains.

They left Maryanne at the terminal with her little suitcase. She would take the next bus back to Philadelphia, she said, where she'd been working in a veterinarian's office. The two embraced loosely, two pale, thin women touching cheeks. "Bye, Ma"—nothing more. Then Maryanne to Harry, in almost a whisper: "I hope it goes okay. You have my cell; please call if anything comes up."

He said that he would, then took Sarah's arm and, with no words between them, guided her toward the exit and his car. She went as willingly as a child.

***

It had begun with an email four weeks earlier, on a Saturday in early May:

> Hello Mr. Harry Hopper:
>
> My name is Maryanne Michaelis. My mother is Ms. Sarah Holmes, who I believe you used to know in Atlantic City, NJ, approx. 25-30 years ago. My mother is sick (also homeless). She has no money and neither do I. She said you might be able to help her. She said that you once told her she was the "love of your life." She said you would remember that. Can you help her? I hope so. I can give you more information when you answer, which I hope will be soon. Thank you.
>
> Sincerely,
> Maryanne Michaelis

Harry had assumed it was a scam. Almost nothing about it felt right: neither surname was the one he remembered; he couldn't conceive of the Sarah he'd known with a daughter (though this meant nothing at all, and he knew it—there were a thousand things about her he'd never known), while the naked pleading seemed almost comical. The "love of your life" line did hit a nerve, as his Sarah would have expected. So the writer may have known her, or known about her. But that proved nothing at all.

The bigger problem was simpler. He didn't *want* it to be real. Sarah was painful history, the living echo of a time and place whose smallest memories still brought an ache. He had deleted the email, and tried to put it out of his mind.

A second one came a week later:

My mother is VERY sick, also kind of crazy. I love her and want to help her, but I can't afford it anymore. She says you used to love her, and might be able to help. I realize that was a long time ago, but I am hoping you'll agree.

Harry wrote back the same day, with as much restraint as he could muster. Yes, of course he remembered Sarah, had "cared deeply for her at one time," and was sorry to hear she wasn't well. He didn't know what he could do to help; he was living on a teacher's salary and had very little to spare. He concluded by proposing a phone call, and suggested a date and time.

***

The voice on the other end was quavering and unsure, but very deliberate and almost without inflection, like a foreigner over-trying her words. But he had known right away it was her.

"Oh Harry, Harry, I'm so happy to hear your voice," was most of what she could manage. She said it twice. They talked for less than a minute. By the time it was over he could feel the phone shuddering against his ear.

Then Maryanne came on. The voice was almost as flat, but slighter, with a tremulousness that hadn't come across in the emails. He asked if Sarah was on drugs. She said yes, that she took pills to sleep: "I don't know what they are, she calls them her 'candy.' I don't know how much she takes, but she's out of it most of the time."

"How do you mean 'out of it'?"

"Like she's half-asleep. She hardly knows where she is. A lot of times she hardly knows me."

"How about physically? Does she have seizures? Does she get sick to her stomach? Can she walk okay?"

"Usually she walks okay, other times like I said, it's like she's half-asleep. And yes she gets sick sometimes, I hear her in the bathroom. I don't know about the seizures, I haven't seen any but I haven't been around that long. But I think she's pretty sick. I worry sometimes that she could die."

***

He never really thought about turning her down. Not in any serious way. And though he would explain it later, truthfully—first to Julia (which he dreaded), and afterward to others—in terms of simple decency, of helping an old friend who'd fallen on hard times (*"Wouldn't you do the same?"*), he knew it was more than that. Sarah was doomed. She'd been doomed the day he met her, and probably long before. You could feel it. It hung off her like a smell.

And for Harry, there was a strange sort of beauty in this: a wing-shot bird, tremblingly beautiful in its struggles to fly. For reasons he could only barely comprehend, he wanted to be close to it. To feel its luster, its cold heat. That was what drew him. It was what had drawn him from the start.

Three

———

He had wanted it all so badly at first. Right from the sunless November morning in 1977, driving east across the South Jersey wetlands in his little green Chevette, when he first caught sight of the fifteen-story, glass-and-steel tower of the half-finished Resorts International Hotel-Casino, gleaming like an ice palace against the gray sky.

He was twenty-six years old, on assignment for the daily in Hartford. New Jersey's gambling referendum had passed the autumn before, though it would be another six months before the first casino would open. But the story already was national news. Legal gambling would be the magic pill for urban blight; Atlantic City, a long-moldering resort of soaring poverty and boarded-up grand hotels, was awaiting its deliverance. "It is the dawn of a new era, and God will be watching," a local pastor had told his flock. The paper wanted a 2,000-word feature on the city's history—its early glory and long, sad decline—along with the "feel" of the place on the eve of its rebirth.

It was colder than he'd imagined for November that far south, with an icy wind blowing in from the ocean. The Boardwalk, which he'd decided would be his first stop (he'd never been on an actual boardwalk before), was nearly deserted that morning, its taffy shops and Skee-ball arcades shuttered for the season, only a few Resorts security guards standing around in doorways to keep out of the cold.

He can still recall every source he met with those two days. There was a developer from Florida (later to be exposed as a mob surrogate, he would turn snitch to stay out of jail), in a dreary, pay-by-the-month office on Atlantic Avenue, who told him of his plans for a condo complex in the Inlet—"the residential jewel of the city," he assured Harry, then made him twice repeat the spelling of his name. A mid-level executive from Caesars Palace in Nevada, tall and severe with streaked blonde hair pasted like a skullcap to her head, whose company had just bought the old Howard Johnson's, was adding seven floors and hundred-plus rooms and would open eighteen months later as the city's second casino. The mayor at the time, Joe Lazarow, a garrulous, thickset, earnest-seeming man, born and raised in the city (the last mayor for fourteen years not to be indicted), who spoke in proud but measured terms of his hopes for its revival. And a dozen or so others: contractors, bartenders, casino execs, a Chamber spokesman, the head of the local NAACP.

The trip's final act was a three-hour dinner with a Cyprus-born urban planner named Angelos Demetriou, who was being paid $1 million for his "master plan" (barely a line of which would ever be adopted), meant to redraw the city around its hotels. Over a meal of stuffed grape leaves and baklava heavily fueled by Greek wine, at a table five floors above the Atlantic (the future site of a $75-a-plate Italian restaurant), he shared with Harry and two other reporters his vision of the future.

"*Think of it, just think of it* . . . Twenty hotels of glass and steel, stretched as far as you can see, like a tapestry, with the ocean embracing it from end to end. A city in harmony with the water it sits on. An American Venice. Can't you just imagine it?"—all this delivered in a silky-rich Mediterranean cadence, with arm-sweeps that took in the Boardwalk and ocean below.

Harry's story, headlined "Second Chance for a Faded Queen," ran in the Hartford paper the following Sunday, on page one below the fold, with a photo of Demetriou, pointer in hand, posing like a new father before a wall map of the city. The first five hundred words recalled the resort's bygone glories:

. . . The city we all know from our Monopoly boards, where our forebears spent weeks at a time in grand hotels with Italianate arches or painted Moorish turrets—The Chalfonte–Haddon Hall, The Traymore, The Marlborough-Blenheim (the latter soon to be imploded to make way for a casino) . . .

This was followed by an account of the city's slow erosion, and current piteous state. "A cross between a ghost town and a ghetto," Harry wrote, "its hotels closed or crumbling, its downtown a six-block strip of shuttered stores, its only theatre a porno house." Then came the section on what he called "The Resurrection," already underway, in which "Three shifts of workers, ninety men to a shift, crawl like ants, twenty-four hours a day, through a fifteen-story neoclassical wonder, recasting it into what will be America's first casino east of Nevada."

The story's coda reeked with exuberance:

Never before in the U.S., at least in modern times, have the hopes of a region turned so utterly on a dime. So many tens of millions of dollars, dumped so seemingly unconditionally on such a long-forgotten backwater. There isn't a life here that isn't being touched . . .

At the time, Harry was prouder of this than of anything he'd written before it. But reading it now, for the first time in years, its grandiosity repels him, while his memory of himself at its writing fills him with a sadness that feels almost physical.

Still, he keeps it, along with scores of others, nearly all of them long forgotten, in yellowed clumps of overstuffed manila envelopes, each one marked by year, in three plastic mail crates in the basement of his house. He thinks sometimes of throwing them out—and once got as far as lugging them to the garage to wait for the recycler. But they are back now where they started, and will probably stay there until he is gone and someone more dispassionate hauls them away.

∗∗

He had been married three years by then. His wife, Anne, a whip-smart, fiery social worker with an unquenchable passion for society's victims, was seven months pregnant and about to go on maternity leave. They had a mortgage and two small car loans.

He had come to understand about himself that he had a hard time sitting still, but had not yet begun to see what the cost of this might be. He was bored. He sometimes felt dead. He lay awake nights often full of fears—they felt almost mortal—of the added anchor of a child. (The two more Anne said she wanted seemed unthinkable.) He feared also, though he couldn't yet let himself say it aloud in his mind, that they wouldn't stay married for long.

Their son, named Woodard after Anne's father—he would forever be Woody to the world—was born on New Year's Day 1978. For Harry, the love was instantaneous. And for a time all-encompassing, like nothing he'd ever known. For the first ten months after his son arrived, it would take nothing more than the sound of his gurgly giggle, or later the sight of his furrowed face as he wobbled like a dying top in his baby-blue stretchies on his odyssey across the living room toward Anne's or his outstretched arms. Harry hadn't known he could love with such completeness, or feel inhabited by anything so pure. And for Anne it was the same—though with her, of course, there was never the sense of surprise.

So for a little while they were a family. They fussed and fretted, and argued over whose turn it was to take Woody for a walk in his stroller—"The lady next door says he has an intelligent forehead," he told his wife once, dead serious, on returning—and talked stupidly about schools and colleges, and whose eyes or chin or ears their little boy might have. And the churning, the fears and the deadness, seemed almost to have lifted.

Then one day it would be Woody's bedtime and Harry would be tired, and have a second or third bourbon or get a call from his editor about a reader's letter disputing some story's facts, or have to listen to Anne tell him again of the homeless addict who'd been keeping her awake nights—and the deadness would be back. And he'd know that it wouldn't be long before it would return full force to reclaim him.

***

He was back in Atlantic City six months later, on the Saturday of Memorial Day weekend 1978 (this time on a freelance magazine assignment), to witness New Jersey's governor cut the ribbon to officially open Resorts. The experience, he would write later, was "like a crowd scene out of a Hollywood disaster film." Two hundred thousand people, some of them waiting since sunrise, backed up a quarter-mile on the Boardwalk to gain entrance to a room the size of an airport hangar with 870 slot machines, sixty blackjack tables, ten craps tables and ten roulette wheels.

Some never made it in. Two women fainted, one of them right next to him; a security guard broke his elbow in the crush; fistfights spilled over from the Boardwalk to the beach. One woman told him she'd driven with her husband all the way from Nashville, had made it inside after six hours in line, then had won two hundred quarters on her first pull of the slots. She was hysterical, careening through the crowd, her plastic bucket of quarters still intact, falling on anyone who'd listen: *"One pull!"* she screamed in Harry's face, both hands around the bucket as though protecting a part of herself. *"One pull! One pull! It's a miracle! Don't tell me it isn't a miracle!"*

Harry had a feeling that morning he'd never had before, or would again: that he could see the future—as clearly as if it were unspooling in front of him like one of those time-lapse videos. He could see the casinos sprouting, one-two-three-four-five-six; the gamblers flooding in on buses, the Boardwalk teeming; the buildings going up and coming down. And the stories. He could see the stories as if he were writing them himself.

He never told Anne of the letter and CV he sent to the *Atlantic City Herald* the week he got home. And when the offer came four months later, he let her believe it was organic, just a matter of the paper needing to beef up its newsroom before the crush of stories that were already coming in. Which, in fairness, was at least partly true.

She may have believed him or she may not have, but it didn't matter in the end. The night he told her of the offer marked, for Harry if not for both of them, the start of their undoing.

It began with incredulity, screaming, obscenities.

"What are you saying? You want to go to *Atlantic City*? You want to go *live* there? You want *us* to live there? Atlantic City's a *shithole*, Harry. You've said so yourself. More than once!"

Things got quieter from there, but no better. He tried to explain. He tried to explain so many things. How they wouldn't be living in Atlantic City itself, that there were towns nearby he could commute from, with good schools and friendly, like-minded people, "not so different from here." How there'd be a real need there, with all the social issues they'd be facing, for a person with Anne's compassion and skills. How Woody was still young enough so he'd feel no real disruption. And how it was a big opportunity for Harry.

"Please try to understand, Anne. What's happening down there, it's like nothing we've ever seen before, like nothing I've ever covered"—and here he paused, and took his wife's hand, which she gave reluctantly, across the little kitchen table where they sat.

"Yeah, the place is a shithole, no question about it. So now they're going to unload these gazillions of dollars on it, all these new jobs and new ways to get rich—and all of it overnight, literally overnight. Can you imagine what that's going to cause? It's going to be like a *bomb exploding.* And that's the beauty of it . . .

"I'm a *reporter,* Anne. But I want to report on something that *matters,* that really matters . . . Does that make any sense to you at all?"

He searched his wife's face for a reaction, much like a doctor might search the face of a patient who's just been given bad news. Her look had softened, but there remained something implacable in it that told him not to be encouraged. After a moment, she smiled at him, a wan smile that felt to him more like kindness than understanding. Then she lowered her head toward her lap and sat very still for what felt like forever.

"Thank you for explaining," she said finally. "And thank you for caring enough to explain."

This confused him. "Of course I care enough," he said.

"Not always," she said. "Sometimes you don't seem to care about very much at all."

He didn't ask what she meant by this, because he knew. They'd been over it before, more than once, though he hadn't expected it now. Not now, not when the subject was their future, whether they would spend it together or apart. He felt a small knot of fear begin to form in his gut.

"I *understand,* Harry," she told him. "Sometimes I wish you weren't such a goddamn dreamer. But I do understand—I really do." She squeezed his hand once, then spoke with a tenderness he hadn't heard in a while.

"I don't want to go to Atlantic City. Or wherever it is you think we'd end up. I don't want it for myself, I don't want it for Woody—for more reasons than I can even think of right now."

She paused for several seconds, fixed her eyes on his, and let out what sounded like something between a gasp and a wheeze. He saw that her eyes were wet. Her voice now was just above a whisper.

"*But I love you,* Harry. I love you, and I love your crazy dreams"—and here she smiled weakly and took his hand again. "I'd do almost anything to support you, I think you know that." She paused again, then took a long breath before continuing.

"But the problem is—the problem is, sometimes it feels like you're already *half gone.* Even when you're here, you're half gone. You know that, don't you?"

"I know what you're going to say, but I don't think it's really fair. I think—"

"You're only *half here*, Harry. You get home as late as you can, you pour yourself a drink as soon as you're in the door, then lose yourself in the paper or some game on TV. We haven't made love in weeks. You never want to go out to dinner, or anywhere on weekends. It's like you wish you were anywhere else, anywhere but here with us. I feel so alone sometimes . . .

"And now you want to really go."

Her words sounded so anguished he felt an almost overwhelming need to hold her, to just pull her close and whisper some sweet blandishments in her ear. Anything to reverse direction before their words took them someplace they couldn't come back from.

He did his best. He said he was sorry, he said he would taper his drinking and try to be more "present" for her and Woody. He said more than this, and they talked for another two hours and shared some difficult truths—he even tried to tell her of the deadness he felt, being careful not to tie it to her or Woody. But in the end "sorry" was most of all he could say. They'd covered the same ground already too many times. There seemed no future now in empty promises.

So the end between them came the way those things so often do between caring people: incrementally, in stages, with sad hopes and good intentions. He would take the job, get a small place near Atlantic City, spend his work weeks there and drive back north on weekends, when they would try their best to be a family. Anne called it their "six-month plan," promising a "re-evaluation" then. But Harry had a strong sense—they both did, probably—of where life would find them once the game had played out.

Four

He started at *The Herald* in January of 1979. The first casino had opened eight months before; the second would follow six months later, with four more to come by the end of the next year. The region, already, was swimming in every kind of pathos he had envisioned: street ministers, bid-rigging politicians, evicted welfare families, pit bosses with law degrees, gamblers and suicides, crusaders and escort services.

Outside of the casinos—which, at least by statute, were overseen by the state—the mob had a piece of most of what went on: the concrete business, the garbage haulers, laundries, building contractors, liquor distributors and limousine companies that serviced the hotels; the boxing promoters who arranged the big-money fights in the casino showrooms, the drug dealers, loan sharks and high-end prostitutes. And at least a few of the offices in City Hall.

And every six weeks or so, a new body would turn up in a car trunk or on a roadside or be pulled from Absecon Bay, as the Philadelphia and New York crime families—Bruno, Gambino, Genovese and others—fought their turf war for control of a city that had been a backwater just two years before.

The Herald newsroom, though, was a sleepy affair. Staffed mostly with old-school, just-the-facts reporters who groused their way between deadlines and seemed to live for their first Irish whiskey at Club Thirty after work—and under a publisher less focused on enterprise than ad lineage—it wasn't a scene that encouraged much initiative. The editor, a coarse, sixtyish old-timer named Alcorn, gobbled cheesesteaks open-mouthed at his desk, dribbled cigarette ashes over reporters' copy and never looked up when he talked, which was rarely. He'd been with the paper thirty-odd years and was counting down the months to retirement. But he hadn't yet lost his instinct for a story. If you could make your case for one, you could be pretty sure you'd at least get a hearing.

One of the first long pieces Harry wrote, less than a month after he got there, seemed to him then (and still does) to stand for much of what the place was about. A twenty-year-old high-school dropout from Kenosha, Wisconsin, named Willoughby, no doubt with a sense of the looming dead ends of his life, had stolen $500 from his big sister's savings account, along with the family's old Camaro, and driven fourteen hours nonstop to Atlantic City to stake it on the outcome of a craps game. He spent the last four dollars of it on the way out of town, on a length of rubber hose. They found him parked in the marshes in Egg Harbor Township, six miles north of the city, dead for a day in the backseat. A note pinned to his shirt read only, "I'm sorry."

***

Harry was at the paper nearly a year before he was assigned his first mob story. It wasn't even current, just an update on a killing that had happened nearly two years before, three months before the first casino opening. The way Alcorn framed it to him, he wondered at the time if he may have felt Harry wasn't ready yet for the real stuff. Either way, he wasn't expecting much.

On the night of February 15, 1978, in the cocktail lounge of the Flamingo Motel on Pacific Avenue, a man wearing a black ski mask and carrying a snow shovel and concealed .22 (the story was legendary already), had walked into the bar unnoticed and fired five bullets into the head and chest of a local judge named Eddie Helfant, who was having dinner with his wife. The killer had escaped in the chaos and the crime remained unsolved.

The assignment was the usual update: any progress on the case (there had been none, though saying so would serve mostly to heighten the effect), a review of the evidence, comments from witnesses (there were about a dozen), theories from Homicide, a word from the wife if he could get one. It was the sort of "Where Are They Today?" feature that predictably gets readership but seldom much of a shelf life.

Harry proposed to Alcorn that he take a different tack: with a slant toward the chief suspect in the case, a mob *capo* and cement contractor named Nicodemo Scarfo, who was rising through the ranks and would win control of Angelo Bruno's Philadelphia crime family—and with it the Atlantic City rackets—two years later. Alcorn said to go ahead and write the piece, that he'd make up his mind when he read it.

The story was a model of indirection. There were references to "unsubstantiated rumors," "unconfirmed sources," an "anonymous spokesman" for the city. The only source named was a Washington-based consultant on organized crime. But it all pointed clearly to Scarfo.

Alcorn cleared it, and it ran on February 15, 1980, the two-year anniversary of Eddie Helfant's killing, under the headline "A *Trail of Riddles: Anatomy of a Judge's Murder.*"

That evening, a Friday, Harry stopped at a liquor store in the mall on his way home from the paper; it was dark by then and snowing lightly.

He returned to his car five minutes later, and had barely sat down before two large, pale hands were on his shoulders, pinning him to the seat. A voice from just behind his head—he never saw the man behind it but could smell the stink of onions and feel his breath on his neck—told him, "Keep your fuckin' head facing forward," then asked him, in a gravelly voice that sounded fake, if he liked his job. Harry said that he did. The voice said that that was good, and that he was "probably a real kickass reporter" but he should be "more careful" what he wrote about. Then he took a piece of paper the size of a business card out of his pocket and handed it to him. Two addresses were scrawled there in pencil: Anne and Woody's in Connecticut, and Harry's in the Chelsea section of the city. The voice said he figured Harry was a "smart young guy," and that he wouldn't want anyone close to him to "get fucked up." Then he took the piece of paper out of his hand and exited the car.

When Harry shared the story in the newsroom, it turned out there were others who'd had such run-ins. One of them, an older, mob-obsessed wire editor named Montgomery who could recite the lineage and "hit record" of every mob family—Colombo, Genovese, Gambino, Bruno, Lucchese, Bonanno and the rest—going back generations, said he thought the guy in Harry's backseat may have been a Scarfo soldier named Rizzo whose specialty was "doing tidy-up errands for his boss." He said he doubted they'd do any "real harm" to a reporter, but advised Harry in the future to "try to write around Scarfo any time you can."

***

When he has thought back on that night since then, as he has more often lately, it always surprises him that it didn't frighten him more. He'd never considered himself any braver than the next person, or as any more of a fool. But the longer he'd thought about it, the more it had come to seem almost comical—the oaf in the backseat with his big hands and his little piece of paper—like some twisted version of the Keystone Cops. But it beguiled him too, in a perverse sort of way, like so much else about Atlantic City in those days.

It was the chaos that drew him. The same sense of crazy, unchecked momentum he'd felt from the start, that he'd tried so hard to describe to Anne: a hurtling toward change that allowed no side-view or sense of history, dispensed casually with victims and embraced mayhem as the price of pace. There seemed to be no one in Atlantic City who had ever read a poem or smelled the dawn.

It was obscene, and over the years he would come more and more to feel its malignance. But for now he felt only its *aliveness*. And already he was almost drunk with it.

Five

———

On a Friday night in early September 1984, two weeks after their first night together at Trump Plaza, Harry called Touch of Class Escorts and asked for "Dawn." She told him she'd meet him again at the Trump bar.

"I have my own room here now," she said, already on her second frozen margarita, when he arrived an hour later. "Starting tonight. You'll be the first to see it." She sounded proud.

"It's really nice, don't you think? Everything is so grand, kind of like you think of a palace. And they're all so friendly. I even got to meet Mister Trump."

Harry hadn't noticed before—the casino bars, in their overdone glitz, all looked the same to him—but now he ordered a bourbon and looked around. The wall behind him was a deep burgundy, broken every several feet by a series of beveled mirrors; the bar itself was backed by a single mirror, ceiling-high, reflecting the bottles and drinkers and tables to the rear. Over it all hung strings of shimmering Tivoli lights in different shapes and colors. There was brass everywhere. The barstools were framed in brass, as were the tables. The bar itself was brass, and reflected off the mirrors and lights in changing shades of green and red. Harry thought of a funhouse.

"It definitely gets your attention," he said.

They had their drinks and went upstairs to a room with lavender walls and a mirrored ceiling. Dawn stayed two hours this time; they smoked a joint together—she had several in her purse—and made love twice. She was as tender as the first time. And there was still that sadness about her.

He asked her real name.

"It's Sarah," she said, "even though you're not supposed to know that"—but wouldn't tell him her surname. When he tried to tease it out of her, she just shook her head no. "That's out of bounds," she said. "Some things are out of bounds."

He asked what else. She paused and looked around the room, then down at her hands. "Oh, just about *everything*," she said, and made a poor attempt at a laugh. "Everything's out of bounds . . . I'm out of bounds, you're out of bounds, the whole world's out of bounds as far as I'm concerned." A sudden somberness came over her as she said this, as though she expected him to know what she meant.

"I guess you're married?" she asked him toward the end of their time. "You seem like the married type."

"What's 'the married type'?" Harry asked.

"Oh, you know, all peaceful and settled down and everything."

"You mean, like, *boring?*"

"Yeah, maybe. Sometimes. But in a good way . . . Actually, I'm not sure what I mean."

He and Anne had been divorced three years by then, and he told her so.

"Do you ever get lonely?" she asked.

"I do sometimes," he said. "How about you?"

"Out of bounds," she answered, but this time with a smile.

He liked her even more than before, for all her boundaries. She was quick, and could be funny, and had a directness about her, a sort of no-nonsense way, which—in combination with the softness that seemed somehow to underlie it—felt irresistible to him.

He asked what she enjoyed when she wasn't working. The answer was so quick it was as though she'd been waiting for the question.

"I like to dance."

"What kind of dance?"

"Rock and roll, oldies, whatever." Her voice had found a new pitch. It was as though he'd flicked a switch.

"Where do you go? Anywhere around here?"

"Memories, mostly. Memories in Margate. You know it?"

He said he'd heard of it, but had never been there himself. What he knew of it, actually, had more to do with the man who owned it than the place itself. Philadelphia DJ Jerry Blavat, widely known as "The Geator," was a long-time Scarfo pal and former driver for Angelo Bruno. A minor legend up and down the Jersey shore, he'd turned the club into a must-go weekend scene for the twenty-something set as well as a lot of aging rockers.

"You like to dance?" Sarah asked him now.

"I used to. But it's been a while," Harry said.

"So you want to go dancing sometime?"

He was shocked by the question. But it was hard not to hear in her voice an echo of her invitation of two weeks before—"So you want to take me to bed?"

"I'm not sure about that," he told her.

There was a pause. Then her eyes narrowed and the lilt disappeared. "Oh. You're worried about being seen with me? Is that it?"

He tried to soften the sound of things: "How can you be sure you won't run into someone from . . . your work?"

She looked at him then, mouth agape, head tilted to one side, in what it took him a second to realize was a caricature of idiocy—then kept it alive with her answer, delivered in what she must have imagined as a Brooklyn patois:

"Whaaaa? Ya think I only got one look? Don't worry, mister, ain't nobody in that place gonna know me!"

Harry laughed. They both laughed. Half an hour later, as he handed her her $150 at the door, she kissed him on the mouth, and said, almost solemnly, "I like you, Harry."

"I like you too," he said.

It was the last time he would pay her.

***

Two Saturday nights later, at ten o'clock, they met at the bar at Memories. Sarah wore a dark red pony tail wig, a worn gray peasant blouse, a pair of ripped jeans and no make-up, not even lipstick. Her green eyes now were brown. She looked nineteen, and lovely. If it's true what they say about falling in love—that there's a single moment, whether you know it or not, when the torch is first lit—that might have been it for Harry.

The dance floor was packed. It was a warm night, just two weeks past Labor Day weekend and crowds at the shore were near their peak. Harry held Sarah's hand to keep from losing her. On a raised stage at the back of the room, The Geator was scanning the floor as he bent over his mixer, a lanky man in his fifties in a Hawaiian print shirt and a crushed black fedora. Then he was looking straight at them, the mic in his hand and the music suddenly down to half its volume:

"Lad-eez and gentlemen—she has arrived! The beyoodeeful dancing queen!" And then with a brief glance at Harry—*"and my man, Pots n' Pans!"*

Sarah laughed quietly and shook her head. This was plainly nothing new. Then The Geator waved at them from the stage and pointed to the turntable in front of him. The volume amped back up. It was Dion's "Runaround Sue," about a broken hearted boy and his two-timing girlfriend.

Sarah tugged at his arm, dragged him onto the floor and began dancing. Within seconds she was somewhere else, some*one* else: eyes closed, lips barely parted, her body moving as though it and the music were all that existed in the world. Harry had never seen such a trans-formation. He stood almost still, gaping, while other couples parted gradually around them.

"*You gotta move!*" she shrieked in his ear over the noise of the crowd. "*You gotta move with the music!*"

And that was how they began—though at the time probably nei-ther of them thought of it as any sort of a beginning. *We enjoy each other*, Harry might have told himself. *There's no one else in my life, and Sarah needs a dancing partner.*

Whatever the thinking behind it, it felt more and more natural as the weeks passed. They'd meet at the Memories bar at ten o'clock any Saturday Sarah wasn't working, and dance till closing time at two. Always The Geator would announce, "*She has arrived! The beyoodee-ful dancing queen!*" And always the first song would be the same. Sometimes she'd come home with Harry afterward, and sometimes (though he always asked) she'd smile, kiss him sweetly and shake her head. He never figured out what went into her decision, and soon learned not to ask.

***

Harry came to love those Saturday nights. He had been in Atlantic City more than five years by then, and had begun to feel oppressed by the filth and falseness of so much around him. Every week brought another account of a bribe or a shakedown or a killing. Six months before their first date at Memories, the city's mayor, Mike Matthews, who had always seemed to Harry like a more than decent man, had been recalled from office and charged with extortion—he would be sentenced to fifteen years in federal prison. His replacement, Jim Usry, would be charged five years later with bribery, conspiracy and official misconduct. The rot was everywhere. And now, if a story going around *The Herald* newsroom could be believed, the paper itself could be a part of it.

Two weeks before, *The Herald's* casino beat reporter, Jack Duffy, a sometime friend and drinking buddy of Harry's, had turned in to Alcorn a story he'd been working on for weeks: Donald Trump, already the owner of the city's premier casino and now in negotiations for a second, had had a string of relationships, going back years, with bosses of the Genovese and Gambino crime families in New York. More recently, he had finalized an Atlantic City land deal with two more mob-connected figures, one of them a scrap-metal dealer described by the FBI as an agent for Nicky Scarfo.

All this should have been grounds for a near-certain denial of Trump's casino license from the state Division of Gaming Enforcement (DGE), which had pledged to root out "even the perception" of mob influence. But the DGE had given Trump a pass—an "unheard-of breach of policy," according to Duffy's story.

He had handed it in to Alcorn on a Thursday afternoon, well under the deadline for the Friday edition. When it didn't run the next day, Alcorn said he was holding it for Sunday, the week's biggest paper. When it didn't run Sunday, Duffy called the editor at home. "We're going to sit on it a while," he was told. "Need to run down some facts."

The story never ran. When Duffy cornered Alcorn in the office a week later, the editor told him the issue was out of his hands.

"He starts in with the old line about how we're lucky to have our jobs at all—how without assholes like Trump we'd all be out on the street," Duffy groused to Harry on a Friday night, over his third or fourth scotch at The Thirty. "But his heart wasn't in it, you could see that, he just kept shaking his head and looking away and saying how it wasn't his decision—that it came from 'upstairs.' He said he thought it was a good story, that maybe I should try to freelance it somewhere else—can you believe it? . . . By the end, I swear, I was actually feeling *sorry* for the guy. He just seemed defeated."

Something began to die inside Harry that night. Lou Alcorn was a good man, crusty and short-tempered and mostly mirthless, but a solid old-style newsman, with all the high-minded principles—Ask the Tough Questions, Play No Favorites, Get the Story Out—that came with it. He was a man you wanted to believe in. And now he was being crushed like a bug. Made to preach a gospel that must have turned everything in him against itself. It was enough to make you want to cry.

More and more, against this creeping moral pestilence that seemed now to come from everywhere at once, Harry found himself drawn into Sarah's sweet orbit. There was something about the rawness of this sad-eyed, wild-dancing young woman, who seemed almost like a girl to him, that touched a place inside him he had almost forgotten was there.

***

After a while they began doing other things. First it was the movies: it was the early days of the multiplex, and Harry called her from work one day and asked if she'd go with him to the one that had just opened in Somers Point, on the mainland. They went the next afternoon and saw three films back to back: *The Right Stuff, The Big Chill* and something or other with Clint Eastwood. Another time, not long after, they rented mopeds at a place in Sea Isle City and rode them half the night till Harry crashed his on a patch of sand and ended up in the ER with two broken fingers—and Sarah blowing kisses from across the room while the doctor splinted them. Once they went bowling in Absecon, where Sarah took instructions from Harry on how to hold and throw the ball, then threw a strike on the first one she bowled—and shrieked like an eight-year-old. Another time they drove north to Six Flags and rode rides and looked at animals all day.

By then, they were spending nights together, either at Harry's place in Chelsea or Sarah's condo in Ventnor—both of them down-beach from Atlantic City—where, when they didn't go dancing or to the movies, they'd eat takeout or cook up burgers or scrambled eggs (neither of them was much at cooking), drink tequilas, watch TV and mess around.

And they talked. Although it would be more truthful to say that Harry talked and Sarah mostly listened—an imbalance Harry tried hard, at least early on, to correct. When he asked her, as he did more than once, to tell him something of her past, of her family and childhood, the people in her life who had mattered, she would offer always different shades of the same paltry details: she'd grown up poor, an only child, in upstate New York, her parents had both died early—she never said how or exactly when—and she had lived after that with an uncle. She had few memories of her parents, she said, and none she would share of her uncle, whom she claimed she never knew well. She had left there in her teens, she said, then lived for a time in Florida and Los Angeles and "a few other places." When Harry asked what she had done there, her answer was like a door slamming shut: *"What do you think?"* she said. And that was the end of that.

There were a couple of funny stories about men she had known, and the time she had inquired idly of Harry, after smoking a joint at his place, "Did you know I went to college?" then typed blazingly ("Now is the time for all good men . . . ") on his Smith Corona as though to prove it. But that was the last he heard of that.

Beyond these few scraps, she dug a moat around her life that he learned, over time, not to try to cross. He had no notion at that point of what troubles might have brought her to do what she did for a living, though he assumed from what little she said—and what she didn't—that there must have been some awfulness. But there was no going there. He willed himself to accept this, and after a while he stopped trying.

So it was mostly Harry who would do the talking. Usually this happened in bed, where, on his days off, they would sometimes linger till mid-afternoon. He told her of his past—his mother's suicide, his father's brittle distance—the jobs he had held, his hopes for the future. He spoke kindly of his wife and lovingly of Woody, admitting that he had been largely to blame for the marriage's failure. He described the hopes he had had for his job at *The Herald*—"I thought this place would be a reporter's wet dream"—but conceded that the near-daily depravity was wearing on him.

Sarah listened raptly. She asked questions about everything, seeming to delight in the smallest details. It was as though he were describing a far-off planet to a curious child.

"Did no one ever read to you, or tell you stories when you were a kid?" he asked her one day. She looked at him blankly, then asked what he meant by stories. "Did you ever have a close friend, or a boyfriend?" he asked then.

"My mommy used to read to me," she said. "At least I think she did, that's what my daddy said. I don't remember, though."

They went out to dinner rarely, always to someplace three or four towns away: Avalon or Wildwood, and once to an old-timey inn in Cape May, the Admiral Benbow, where they ate at a table overlooking the beach. Sarah was quiet through much of the meal, watching an old man with a metal detector, in a wool hat and parka (it was winter by then) illuminated only by the inn's light, passing back and forth over the same fifty yards of sand. The waiter said he was there at the same time several nights a week, and had been for as long as anyone could remember, walking different lengths of sand in the same half-mile of beach. No one knew what he was looking for, or even if he knew himself. There was a rumor that his wife had flung her wedding ring across the beach years before, in an argument before they parted, and that he believed that finding it would win her back.

Sarah cried when she heard the story. She asked the waiter if he knew the old man's name. He said he didn't. Then she asked Harry if he'd go with her, right then, to talk with him. Harry said he'd rather wait until after their dinner—and that was the first real argument they had. The man was gone by the time their dessert came, and they had never been back.

For whatever reasons—and he wasn't sure himself—he was mostly untroubled by how she made her living. At least in those early days. Partly, he guessed, because sex for pay was how they'd gotten started, so it had come to seem unremarkable to him. Probably also because there was never any talk of a future, by either of them, which made moral judgments more or less moot.

***

In early June of the second summer—1985—they started going to the beach. They went always on a weekday, and would choose between one of the towns farther down the coast where the crowds were thinner and Sarah was less likely to be recognized (though she still wore a wig—she called this one her "beach hair"). She'd never learned to swim, but seemed to enjoy just being in the water, and never cared how cold it was. Harry tried to teach her to body-surf, though her efforts there were mostly comical: She invariably mistimed the waves or got swept under and came up snorting like a horse, her nose full of water and her face in a cartoonish moue. But she never gave up trying.

One memory of those months he never tires of replaying.

It was July or August of that same summer. He was sitting on the beach in Stone Harbor, midway between the boardwalk and the water, watching Sarah trying to stay afloat on a medium-sized wave. She almost managed it this time, toppling over herself only at the last second as the wave broke and delivered her to the beach. In an instant, she was on her feet, sprinting toward him, her wig hair matted across one side of her face, her small breasts half out of the top of her yellow-and-green two-piece.

"*Almost!*" she screamed at him as she ran, her arms pumping the air, her mouth puckered in a tiny O. "Almost! Almost! Almost!"

There's no accounting for what Harry did next. But in that moment, in the small, silly joy of witnessing this picture of delight, he was moved to somewhere beyond himself.

"*Yes, almost!*" he yelled back, and began clapping showily. She beamed up at him, did a little half-pirouette, then turned and threw herself sideways onto the sand and lay there, head back, shrieking her joy.

His eyes teared. He straightened his arms in her direction, palms facing toward her in a signal to wait, then ran down to just past the wave-line, fell on his knees on the wet sand and scrawled his impossible message—fast, with his knuckles in two-foot letters:

U R THE LUV OF MY LIFE

He looked up at her. She was sitting now, arms hugging her knees, seeming to smile. Then she jumped up, scampered down to within a few feet of him, went down on all fours and wrote her answer. She smiled as she wrote it, then peered up at him, squatting on her haunches. Her face was cold-mottled; the hairs on her arm stood straight as little pins:

U R FULL OF SHIT

He adored her for that.

"You're beautiful," he said.

"Thank you," she answered. "And you're full of shit."

***

But so often, like that day, there would come a contradiction.

Minutes later, at an ice cream stand on the boardwalk, wrapped tight as a mummy in a bright orange beach towel, a snow cone half-eaten in her hand, she had begun, almost soundlessly, to cry.

"Do you ever feel like you're a character in a movie, then remember all of a sudden that you're not?" was all she would say in explanation.

Something in the suddenness of her tears, like a cloud passing over the sun where there had been no cloud in sight, filled him with a sudden dread. But he only smiled, stroked her hair and let it pass. He'd grown used to her riddles by then.

"It's all right," he said. "It's nothing so terrible. We all feel like actors sometimes."

She was a mystery to him, this child of a woman he was coming to love. Almost daily, she confounded him with her strangeness: so seemingly unbounded, yet so in thrall to feelings that could level her at any moment. He marveled at this, when it didn't frighten him.

***

Like most children, she set much stock in birthdays. On Harry's, in early July, she had bought a cake and hidden two small presents, then made a game of his search for them, cuing him, "warmer . . . colder," until he found one under each bra cup. Then she'd taken him out to dinner and had the waiter bring an ice cream pie with a relighting candle, giggling softly behind her napkin as he futilely puffed.

Sarah's birthday was a month later, in August. It was one of the few bits of data Harry had gleaned from her—though she was coy about her age. That morning, he called a florist and arranged for delivery of a dozen yellow roses to her condo at five o'clock; she would be working that night, and would have to be gone by dark. When the time came, he bagged two splits of champagne and a small jade necklace he'd once seen her admire, and set off on foot to her place.

The flowers hadn't arrived yet when he got there. The two of them sat together on the little couch while Sarah opened the box with the necklace: pale green, carved in the shape of a tiny elephant with ame-thyst gemstones for eyes.

"*You remembered!*" she said, plainly delighted. "I'm not used to get-ting presents—I don't even know how long it's been." And she reached over, wrapped her arms around Harry's neck and held on.

"Elephants are good luck in India," he said when she released her hold. "Maybe he'll bring you some."

They were still on the couch, fastening the clasp at the back of Sarah's neck, when there came a shrill squawk from the kitchen. Sarah jumped as though from a gunshot.

"Someone's in the lobby. *Oh, God,* not now." She moved jerkily toward the intercom, but Harry got there before her.

"Relax, I'll handle it." He smiled—mischievously enough, he hoped, to reassure her. Her eyes rolled in relief.

"Roses, man. A dozen big yellows." The man in the doorway was Black, about thirty, and not much taller than Sarah, but with a chest that stretched the weave of a green acrylic sweater in a manner meant to be noticed. He was gap-toothed but handsome, with a face pocked by small divots. His smile was broad and open, the kind that asked for a smile in return.

"Your name's Hopper, right?"

Sarah, still seeming almost frozen, murmured from the background: "*Roses, Harry? You brought me roses?*"

He started to answer, but the other man cut him off: "Looks like he did, ma'am," he said, then bestowed the flowers with a small flourish

on Sarah, at the same time winking sideways at Harry, who paid him—
$40—thanked him, and told him to keep the change.

"Thank you, man, I appreciate that . . . And anytime you get
the urge for flowers—or balloons, we got balloons too, all sizes, all
colors—you just call and ask for me personally. Ask for Tyrone, like
Cyclone, and I'll get 'em to you, wherever you at. Won't be no delays
with—"

"*Tyrone?* Your name's *Tyrone?* They call you Cyclone?"

Sarah, who had been standing between the two of them, holding the roses in both hands like a choirboy, was now riveted on the
deliveryman.

"Yes, ma'am, that's the name all right."

"Tyrone *Everett?*"

"Yes, ma'am." The man stared at Sarah, his smile now stunted by
confusion.

"You were a boxer, right?"

The man had backed up several steps. He seemed suddenly guarded.

"Yes, ma'am. Used to box at Resorts, couple of years back. You see
me fight?"

"No, but I heard about you. You were good."

"Number Eight for a while, had a shot at Number Four. But thank
you kindly, I appreciate that. You a fight fan?"

"No, we just know some of the same people, is all." Sarah smiled at
the man, her face full of kindness, meant to reassure. "I heard how good
you were, though. Maybe you can go back to it. You know what they
say—it's never too late."

The man looked at her, the puzzlement on his face making him
seem almost comical. Harry was transfixed now, his look swiveling from
one of them to the other, like a child trying to decipher the banter
between adults.

"That ain't too likely, ma'am. If you know anything about why I got out, then probably you know that ain't too likely."

"I know something about it. . . . But I understand. You have to do what's best for you."

"Yes, ma'am."

The man began to back toward the door, plainly uncomfortable. Sarah moved quickly—"Hold up a second, Tyrone, will you?"—walked past him and into the bedroom, returning moments later with what Harry could see were two fifties.

"I want you to have this," she said to him in what was almost a whisper. They were standing together by the door. "As a gift. And think about what I said—it's never too late."

The man took the money uncertainly, then stared at it as though he'd just opened his fist and found it there.

"Do I *know* you?"

"We've never met, I promise. But I'm glad we have now. And thanks for bringing the flowers."

"Thank *you*, ma'am. I ain't real sure what this is for"—he gestured at the bills as though they were plutonium. "But I do thank you. And for the kind words as well."

He backed the final steps to the door, nodded once to each of them, and was gone.

***

"I'm sorry, but I'm lost. Would you mind telling me what that was about?"

"Oh, it's the same old stuff." Sarah seemed suddenly remote, as though waking from a dream. "I've just heard about him, is all. He gets mentioned sometimes." She was scrabbling around now in a kitchen cabinet, looking for something to use as a vase.

"Mentioned how?"

"He was supposed to lose a fight, I think, and he didn't—or couldn't, I don't know. Anyway he won, and they'd all bet on the other guy or something. So they screwed him."

"Who's 'they'?"

"Who do you think, Harry? I'm sure you can figure it out."

"Okay. So how'd they screw him?"

"The way they do. They put him out of business. He just stopped getting fights. That's how they do it—you wake up one day and you're done, you're finished, no one'll talk to you anymore. It's like you never existed. Either that or they hurt you. Whatever they want to do to you, however they want to get back."

She had located a mason jar by now, and was pouring water for the roses, although she seemed barely to notice them.

This was new territory, for them both. Sarah had rarely talked about anything that involved what she called her "other life." And while Harry had assumed there might be a mob connection with Touch of Class, it seemed unlikely that it would extend to her. He had asked lamely once or twice about her clients: Were there politicians, any-one with a face or name she knew? Her answers were always the same: that she rarely paid attention to anything they said, including the fake names they gave her, and forgot their faces by morning.

"So how come the guy's still around?" he asked now.

"He's from here, I think. He trained here, at some gym in the Inlet. I heard he still goes there, that it's like a home to him. They laugh when they talk about that. So sad—"

And here she stopped—to catch herself, it seemed—then contin-ued in the same half-dreamy tone.

"He was good. People knew him. So today, anytime they get a fighter gives them trouble, they always say the same thing—that he'd better straighten up or he'll end up like the Cyclone."

It confused Harry to hear her talk so passionlessly. There was no trace of fear or anger, and none of the feeling she'd shown with the boxer. It was clear the encounter had tripped some nerve, though there was no way of knowing what or why. Or how she knew what she knew.

**

The rest of the evening seemed meant for small comforts. It had begun to rain, and would continue through the night, a gray, steady patter that skittered against the windows like the sound of faraway drumming and would turn the streets to small lakes by morning. Harry scrambled some eggs and mixed mimosas. Sarah seemed only half there.

They sat down together on the floor, their backs against the couch, facing the never-used little fireplace, Sarah absently sniffing the roses next to her in their makeshift vase—Harry has never since been able to smell fresh roses without remembering that evening. They talked about quotidian things: Harry about a story he was working on—how a young Black welfare family had been burned out of their Inlet tenement and now were living on the street. Sarah said she still read everything he wrote for *The Herald*, and that she thought he had a "real feel for people."

Toward the end of the evening, shortly before he planned to leave— Sarah was expected at nine o'clock for her first job of the night—Harry asked her, as off-handedly as he could manage, the question that had been banging around in his head.

"That Tyrone guy, you think he'd talk to me?"

"About what?"

"Things in general. His background, his career, maybe why he's delivering flowers instead of fighting."

"So you could write a story about it, you mean?"

It stung him to hear her say this, though it was most of what he had in mind. But his reasons were too complicated to even think about trying to explain. So he said the only honest thing he could.

"Maybe. But there's more to it than that."

"Tyrone's lost everything he ever dreamed of. That's the only story there is . . . I don't want to talk about him anymore."

So they didn't. Which was nothing new—just another dark, unexplorable corner in a life made up of them. Which worried Harry a little when he let it. But the truth of it was (though he wouldn't think of it this way until long after) that there was something about it all—the unexplained secrets, the dark clouds, the danger—that excited him, that made him feel alive.

***

And so, for more than a year—from the summer of 1984 to the September that was now a month away—the two of them, without questioning much at all, danced and rode mopeds, went to movies, beaches and amusement parks, drank tequila and enjoyed one another's bodies. It was the last time in Harry's life he remembers as anything you'd call blissful.

Six

———

June 2017

At least once a day for the first week after she arrived on her bus, Sarah would thank Harry for his kindness and make him promise she wasn't "too much trouble." She apologized for everything. Sometimes she cried. When he asked her about her life the last thirty years—Where had she lived? How had she managed? Did she have any friends she could call on?—usually she would just shake her head slowly and look away.

Once he had tried to make a joke of it: "So I guess all that stuff's *'out of bounds,'* huh?" But she just looked at him oddly, as though he were speaking another language. She seemed almost a stranger to him. Except for the memories, which kept coming back in flashes he didn't know what to do with.

Those first few weeks spooled out mostly as a jumble of names and dates and a gibberish of opinions, nearly all of them different. An internist, a pain specialist, a neurologist, a gastroenterologist, a dentist, a psychologist, a substance abuse counselor, a masseuse, a Tibetan Buddhist teacher.

And the trips to the department store, the shoe store, the pharmacy, the hairdresser, Walmart for a table fan, the grocery store twice a week. Harry had found Sarah a clean motel room with a queen bed, sofa, microwave and mini-fridge, for $260 a week, less than twenty minutes from his house. When he first brought her to see it, she collapsed in his arms and cried.

He got her qualified for Medicaid, which covered part of it. But even with that the cost to him, the first month alone, was nearly $4,000. He'd mentally allotted $10,000 total, and had no plan (and really no recourse) if the number went higher.

She was addicted to oxycodone, used several other drugs sporadically and was probably an alcoholic. She had a bottle of about two hundred 20mg pills stuffed inside an old yellow towel in her suitcase; Harry had made her show him when he booked her into the motel. She told the doctor she was taking "three or four" a day. There was no way of knowing what the truth was, but her speech was thick and often halting, she was nearly always tired, and it seemed to take nothing to confuse her. She had "mild-to-moderate" kidney disease, which the doctor said should be monitored and might be controlled with diet. There was also a heart arrhythmia, and the GI tests they ran showed damage to her stomach wall. The neurological tests were inconclusive, other than to reveal some memory loss and a slight tremor. All things considered, things could have been worse.

***

The Buddhist teacher had been Julia's idea. Certain Buddhist practices, she told Harry, had made a difference in the lives of some of the homeless she had studied. Julia, who had known almost nothing of Sarah, and who Harry had feared might feel resentful of her sudden arrival on the scene, once again surprised him.

"Did you love this woman?" she had asked, in her particular

straight-ahead way, when he had told her of Sarah's plight and of their history together—omitting its most damning details—and of his plan to try to help her. They were at dinner in Boston's North End; it was a week before Sarah's planned arrival.

He said yes, that he had.

"And do you still?"

He said that he didn't, that they'd been out of touch for years, he'd sometimes wondered if Sarah was even still alive.

"Do you think you're going to save her?" Julia asked then. But there was less challenge in her voice than concern.

"Honestly, I don't know. I don't really see myself as the savior type."

"I'm glad to hear that."

"But she's sick, she doesn't have a dime, and there's no one else in her life outside of her daughter, who doesn't seem like much of a savior either."

Harry hadn't expected the next question.

"So when do I get to meet her?"

***

Ten days later, on what was to be Sarah's first big shopping trip—for shoes, a raincoat, some new jeans, a decent blouse or two—the three of them met at Harry's house on a Saturday morning. Julia greeted Sarah with a hug. Sarah, wide-eyed and as skittish as a child, seemed to shrivel at her touch. It was an awkward beginning.

The mall was thirty minutes away. Sarah, in the back seat of the car in a pair of jeans and the same old blue turtleneck she'd arrived in, sat pressed against the door, her eyes fixed on the road outside. To any question or comment directed her way—nearly always from Julia—she responded with polite mumbles.

Julia, finally defeated, began shuffling through a stack of CDs: The

Stones, Sugarland, Willy Nelson, Norah Jones, Mariah Carey, some others. After a while she handed the stack back to Sarah.

"You a fan of any of these?" Harry doubted that she was. She didn't seem a fan of much of anything anymore.

Half a minute passed; Julia glanced over at him, smiled and shrugged. Then the answer came back. It was small and shy, but so full of delight he felt himself shiver—the first time since she'd arrived he'd heard anything in that voice that didn't sound like defeat:

"*This one*," Sarah said. "Lucinda Williams. Do you know 'Side of the Road'? I love this song *so much*."

Julia popped it in. Harry waited several seconds, then glanced in the mirror as the song came on—about a young woman, staring across a field at a farmhouse, wondering who might live there and if they loved each other. Sarah's eyes had closed, her head was tilted back against the seat, her brow furrowed deeply, lips moving with the words.

It was like looking at a ghost: the goofy, off-kilter smile, the possessed concentration, "Runaround Sue" or Madonna's "Like a Virgin" pumping its rhythms through the rafters of a packed South Jersey club at one a.m. on a weekend night half a lifetime ago. Only the song now was as different as the time—a country singer's melancholy ode to love and domesticity.

What was Sarah's connection to this song? What did it have to say to a sixty-year-old drug addict just out of a halfway house? Was it a memory or an aspiration?

Harry never got a chance to ask. The last lines were playing, Sarah still somewhere far away, as they turned into the entrance to the mall.

***

Julia cooked dinner that night at Harry's place. Sarah's mood had held up. She was still mostly quiet, but seemed comfortable enough now, more than willing to be a part of things. They talked about music, food, cats—Sarah said she'd had one named Bobby, "before I got in trouble with the police"—her love of circuses and county fairs (Harry vaguely recalled something like this), a friend named Pam she knew from the halfway house and hoped to reconnect with before too long.

And finally, toward the end of the evening, her daughter Maryanne, whom she'd rarely mentioned up to then. Harry knew only that Maryanne had been born sometime around 1988, that she'd been the result of a "short thing" with a race-car driver who died on the track not long after she was born, and that Sarah had given her up for adoption. Some years later—it was never clear when exactly, but likely in Maryanne's teens—she had "rescued" her from a foster family, and they'd lived together "off and on" for the first several years, then again later, until the time of the email and the bus trip north. This account had more holes than answers, and there was no telling if parts of it were even true, but it was all Harry had been able to coax out. It did seem to him, though, from what Sarah said and the tender tone behind it, that there was a bond there.

Julia had a daughter also, about the same age, studying in Rhode Island to be a veterinarian. Sarah told her what she knew about Maryanne's s job—which wasn't much, other than that it was in a veterinarian's office—and the two of them mused for a while on the randomness of things.

For Harry it was like watching a play. He had felt this since that afternoon in the car: two strangers, brought together from different chapters and times—different worlds, with him the only bridge—to act out their scripted scenes. He ached for both of them. Half of him was riveted. The other half wanted to run from the room.

None of them drank anything stronger than ginger ale, in deference to Sarah, from whom Harry had extracted a promise to stay away from liquor until they could get more direction from the doctor. (The pills were another matter; she wouldn't even talk about quitting those.) Almost nothing was said all night, at least directly, about her current troubles. And Atlantic City was understood to be a black hole. Through dinner and the hour that followed, none of them went near it—which, for Harry at least, only increased its power in the room.

Until finally, for Sarah, who he could see was getting more tired by the minute, the strain must have been too much.

She and Julia were sitting next to each other on the couch, still talking about their veterinarian–daughters, when Julia mentioned that hers, a warm, sympathetic young woman named Faith whom Harry had met several times and liked very much, was to be getting married in September. It would be a good-sized wedding, Julia said; she hoped there wouldn't be a big to-do with her ex about the cost.

"Will there be dancing?" Sarah asked suddenly.

"Oh, I think so, yes," Julia said.

"So you'll be dancing too, Harry?"

Harry said he expected he would be, then tried to reroute the conversation.

"Harry never used to like to dance much," Sarah said to Julia, but still with a playfulness in her tone.

"*Really?*" Julia said, and laughed, though Harry caught a quick glance in his direction. "Well, in this case he may not have much choice."

"I used to have to *drag* him onto the floor"—and now he heard something else in her voice. "Remember that, Harry? At Memories? With—with The Geator? I'd have to pull and plead and all before he'd give in and get out there with me."

Harry didn't remember it that way, and said so. He tried some weak humor, something about the oaf he was on the dance floor, but there was no heading her off now and he knew it.

"So you two go dancing sometimes?"

Julia said that they'd been once or twice.

Sarah turned to Harry and snorted. "What's wrong with you, Harry? You don't want to *please your woman?*"

"Nothing to do with pleasing anyone," he said, as cooly as he could manage. Then, far too quickly: "Come on, Sarah, it's getting late, I'll drive you back to your place."

She knew she was being dismissed. Her lower lip trembled, her face shriveled—exactly as it always had, exactly as he remembered—and he was sure she was going to cry. He felt something inside him turn over.

She didn't cry, though her face contorted gruesomely in her effort to hold it back.

"No, no, no—it's not that, it's not that . . . You don't want to please your woman, that's what it is . . . You don't want to please—"

Julia moved toward her, put a hand on her shoulder, then began to wrap her in a hug. Sarah pushed her off, but not with much force.

"No, no, don't, please don't—"

For the next minute or so the three of them just sat there, facing each other, Julia and Sarah on the couch, Harry in the chair a couple of feet away. Sarah's head was in her hands now; Julia had one hand still on her shoulder. It seemed to last an hour: a still-life, a moment frozen between outcomes.

Then Sarah raised her head. Her eyes were clear now, her mouth a straight line.

"I shouldn't have come," she said, so quietly Harry could almost not hear her. "It was the wrong thing to do—the wrong thing to come, and I knew it."

Harry started to protest, but Sarah shook her head. She was quiet after that. They all were. Julia hugged her; she allowed it this time but only barely responded. Another minute went by. Then Sarah got up slowly from the couch without a word, looked at Harry and walked to the door. He followed her outside to the car.

***

All the way back to the motel, Sarah sat with her head down and her hands in her lap. When he couldn't bear the silence anymore, Harry said the only thing he could think of:

"It's going to be all right. We're going to make it all right."

She nodded but didn't answer. When they got to the motel—*The Ebb Tide, Truckers Welcome*—he parked in the spot nearest her room but left the engine idling.

"Julia likes you," he told her. She didn't answer. She didn't seem to have heard.

They sat there in the dark, in the silence. Half a minute went by. From somewhere down the long row of rooms a door opened and closed, a car's headlights went on, then off again. Harry could barely see Sarah's outline in the seat next to him. Then he heard her sigh.

"Well, *here we are*," she said finally. "Here we are, at another motel, huh? We did pretty good at some of those, didn't we?"

But she said it without expression, and her head hadn't moved. She was sitting stiffly upright, staring ahead.

Harry said nothing.

Then she spoke again: "Julia's a—a nice lady. I like her."

"That's good," he said. "She likes you too."

Once again, silence. He was about to get out of the car, help her out and take her to her door. But something held him.

"You oughtta take her dancing," she said.

Another long pause, even longer this time, as the dark and the silence seemed to take on weight around them. Harry thought of a bag lady he'd once interviewed for a story; he wondered what had become of her, tried to remember what she'd told him of her past. He thought of Sarah in the Trump bar the night he met her, of her wild joyousness on the dance floor, of the night she'd sat there making faces and blowing him kisses while they set his broken fingers at three a.m. in the emergency room in Cape May.

"This is weird, huh?"

"Yes, kind of."

He didn't know what else to say. Then he got out and took her to her door. When they got there, they stood very close, almost touching; the only light, dim and far above, was from the street behind them. Harry could feel the strands of Sarah's hair, limp and silvery blue in the darkness, grazing his cheek. She smelled of lavender soap.

"You're still handsome, Harry," she said after a moment. "I wondered if you would be. And you are."

He felt his chest heave. He pulled her to him, buried his face in her hair then drew it back to within an inch of hers. Her eyes were staring up at him, wide and wet with tears. She didn't blink or flinch.

"We were *so young*," she said. "So young. I've always wished—" and here she stopped and lowered her head to his chest. He felt her small sobs judder against his breastbone.

It was too much for him. He cried. They cried together. For what felt like interminable minutes, and for reasons probably neither of them fully understood—love, loss, guilt, memory, the waste of lives and years—they held tight to one another. Cried themselves out, both of them quaking, Sarah's tears drying in the weave of Harry's shirt and his in the limp, brownish gray of her hair.

"We never even took a picture, did we?" she whispered through sniffles at the end. "Remember that little photo place on the boardwalk in Stone Harbor? You wanted to go in and take a picture, but I wouldn't. I was too scared. Remember that?"

He did remember, and said so.

"But now we're old and it's like it all never happened, you know?"

"*It happened, Sarah. We happened.*"

And he took her face in his hands, pulled it to his and kissed her—gently, then more deeply, until he felt her return it, with just enough force and movement to tell him that she remembered, too. They held each other for what felt like a long time, until Harry felt the quakes begin to subside.

He kissed her again, lightly this time, dropped his hands from her shoulders, and half-walked, half-ran toward the car. He felt her eyes on him from where he'd left her standing, alone in the dark at her door.

Seven

———

The Lucky Lady Gym stood like a ragged fortress at the north end of New Jersey Avenue. Known once simply as Toby's Gym before casinos came to town, and before that the home of the Mount Zion Baptist Church, it was today the only building left on a flattened block of former row houses peopled mostly at night by addicts and patrol cars. A cavernous, gray brick rectangle of warehouse design—single-story, with a door at its center—its cheerlessness as a church must have seemed an affront to the neighborhood when there still was one. But it had long since outlived its detractors.

It was two weeks before Harry could get there, on a morning in mid-September. He had driven by it in the past, but had never paid it much notice or thought to go inside—which he saw right away had been a mistake. The main room alone, he could see at a glance, had some stories to tell. Yawning and high-ceilinged, with gray-painted concrete walls and windows too high for either view or ventilation, it had once been the church's nave. An industrial fan, half the size of a helicopter's blade-span, rotated noisily from the ceiling. The floor was of rough wood, darkened at perfect horizontal intervals where the pews had once crossed it; canvas mats of various shapes were now strewn at all angles from end to end.

Along one wall, several tight leather speed bags hung from boards whose steel supports were riveted into concrete wall beams. Near the center of the room, two heavy canvas bags hung by ropes from the ceiling.

There were a dozen or so boxers there the day he arrived, plus three or four grizzled older men who looked to be trainers. All were Black. The boxers, who ranged from their late teens to probably close to forty, moved in a slow, staggered flow between training stations—speed bag, heavy bag, jump rope, free weights—seemingly indifferent to each other, and to Harry. The air was a mix of sweat and liniment. The sense of work was palpable.

The ring, the focal point of it all, sat alone at the front of the room in the narrow alcove that once held the altar, the farthest point from the door. It was a twenty-foot square with stretched canvas flooring. Dirty towels hung from the ropes on three sides; the fourth backed up to the wall. It was the first ring Tyrone Everett had ever seen, or boxed in—at six years old, he would tell Harry later—and the only one left to him now.

There were two men he'd come to see that day. The first was Tyrone, who he'd learned (just as Sarah had said) was still a regular at the gym, despite no longer having a career to train for. Harry was hoping he could build some trust with him. He wasn't sure what might come of that—maybe a story, maybe nothing at all—but it might at least open up a glimpse into Sarah's world.

The other was Toby Ward, a former ranked welterweight out of Philadelphia (where they'd known him as Sweet Sultan) who'd run the gym as long as it had been a gym, close to thirty years by then. Whatever stories there were to tell, he figured to be the one to tell them.

Most of what Harry knew of Toby he'd gotten from *The Herald's* archive, in a two-year-old story by a sports reporter Harry used to pal around with. According to that, Ward, a "surrogate father" to most of the boxers in the gym, had started it in the late '50s, just after the church shut down, when land in the Inlet could be had for almost nothing.

"The local kids would come around," he had told the paper, "some of them no older than six or seven. Idea was, get them off the street, teach them to box a little, try to get them to believe in themselves."

Over the next twenty years he taught half the boys in the Inlet to box. For many, he was the only father they'd known; for a few, sometimes for months at a time, the only source of room and board. In 1968 the mayor presented him with a plaque and the keys to the city. The plaque, which cited Ward's "selfless devotion to the young men of the North Inlet" and featured an enameled black-and-white photo of him as a crouching young welterweight in trunks and gloves, hung still on a wall in the gym's locker room.

Then casinos came to town and began hosting pro fights. First Resorts, then The Sands and The Tropicana. And now Trump Plaza, which was hosting some of the biggest. This had brought a call for training space, then for local fighters. Toby's offered both of these, and the managers had come around, bringing their boxers and recruiting the gym's better ones, including Tyrone, to fight on undercards in the casino showrooms, promising them purses usually far greater than anything they would ever see.

Before long, according to *The Herald* story, "The pros' training began to interfere with the kids and the amateurs," and Ward had moved to limit it. Several months of haggling had followed, before Resorts, the company with the deepest pockets, had made him an offer he couldn't turn down—and the gym became The Lucky Lady, though the locals all still called it Toby's.

But it was a different place after that. Kids weren't allowed anymore: you had to be sixteen now to train there, and amateurs were discouraged unless they were training to be pros. And while Ward was kept on to run the place, he almost never coached anymore, or sparred or gave rubdowns or held the big bag for fighters—there were handlers now to do those jobs. So he just cleaned up and kept an eye on things.

There was no mention in *The Herald* of how much Resorts had paid for the place, but Harry had noticed a new Oldsmobile Cutlass on the street outside that could only have been Ward's. So it seemed likely he'd done all right.

That story had run in early '82, two weeks prior to Tyrone's last fight, and had mentioned him prominently:

. . . *the pride of the gym, and Toby Ward's prize pupil, eighth-ranked middleweight Tyrone ('Cyclone') Everett, with a record of eleven wins, one loss, will fight next month at Resorts against unranked newcomer Esteban Castillo (3-1-1).*

Tyrone had won that bout, on a unanimous decision, then had never fought again. This seemed in line with what Sarah had told Harry, which of course made him want to know more.

***

Tyrone wasn't hard to find. In black satin trunks and a sleeveless gray sweatshirt with the Resorts logo across the front, he was by himself in the center of the room, hitting the big bag with a savagery Harry could only imagine against the body of an opponent. He was sweating heavily; his arms, glistening at every crevice, moved against the bag with the perfect rhythm of right-angle pistons. Harry was reminded for a moment of an oil painting he'd once seen of John Henry laboring against the steam drill. He watched until he'd finished, hitting the bag with a final right hand so ferocious Harry felt his stomach tighten.

He had seen by then the films of two of Tyrone's fights at Resorts— both wins—and was amazed at how easily he commanded the ring. His quickness was stunning, his counterpunch so instantaneous it seemed more reflex than reaction. He'd showed no signs of tiring, and seldom clinched or retreated. At times he could appear reckless, stalking an opponent in a kind of dance-step, his hands dangerously low—but he was usually too quick for anyone to take advantage. His talent was beyond question.

"Hey, Tyrone, how're you doing?"

"Who're you?"

"Couple weeks ago? A dozen roses? The Ventnor condo?"

"Oh, yeah, man. How you doing?"

But he seemed indifferent, and began moving toward the weight bench. It occurred to Harry that the gym may not have been the best choice of meeting spots.

"You look tough on that bag. You do that every day?"

"More than once."

"You were a hell of a middleweight, I heard. Eleven wins, a bunch of knockouts."

"Six total, four straight"—but now with a small grin.

"My name's Harry Hopper, I'm with *The Herald*. Maybe we could talk sometime?"

"Never heard of you," Tyrone said. Now at the weight bench, he was assessing the load on a bar Harry figured was at least 300 pounds—"So what you want to talk about?"

Harry started to tell him, but Tyrone cut him off.

"Who was that *lady* you was with? That was the biggest tip I ever got, man, a hundred dollars. What was that about?"

Harry was ready for this. "Like she told you, Tyrone, that wasn't a tip, it was a *gift*. She's a friend of mine. She told me about you, said you were a good fighter who got a lousy break. She's had a few of those herself."

"You talkin' in riddles, man. So how come she know so much about me?"

"You know some of the same people, that's all. It's a long story, like yours probably. But it's not what I came to talk about. How about we talk about boxing?"

Tyrone shook his head, then looked up at the ceiling.

"Why me?"

"From what I hear, you're about the best boxer ever came out of this town. I figure that makes you a pretty good place to start."

Tyrone was straddling the weight bench now, his hands folded at his crotch, looking up at Harry through half-closed eyes. Harry felt he was being measured. Then the eyes opened, the lips parted and curled over uneven teeth—and there was that big open grin from two weeks before.

"A dozen big yellows. And a *hundred-dollar tip*. She must be *some* kinda lady . . . So tell me what you want from me, man."

"I'd sure like to see you box."

He was getting ready to say more, but there was no need. Tyrone clapped his hands once, leapt from the weight bench as though released by a spring and was across the floor, almost in a single motion. Then he was through the ropes and into the ring, twirling a pair of balloon-sized gloves by their laces from the center of the canvas—a half-naked drum major—issuing his challenge to the room:

"Which of you slow-moving dudes wants to be ducking The Cyclone's lightnin' jab this morning?"

He did a quick mimicry of a three-punch combo—*pop-pop-BOOM*— then switched to a caricature of a terrified opponent: high-stepping clockwise around the perimeter of the ring, arms sheathing his head as though from shrapnel, peering backward over his shoulder every several steps, eyes wide as little saucers, his face a burlesque of horror. A near-perfect riff on the young Muhammed Ali.

All movement in the gym had stopped. The boxers were an audience now: laughing or head-shaking or booing in mock derision, as delighted as a roomful of school kids. The performance ended, the group erupted in a sing-song of canted jive, the boxers taunting and hooting, the handlers making bad jokes about windless cyclones and Geritol jabs. Someone yelled out something about rocking-chair match-ups for old fighters who can't quit. Tyrone answered this with a burlesque of an ancient boxer on a cane, then punched the air in another mock-combo and laughed like a Santa Claus.

The affection behind all this was as obvious as the humor; it was plain that Tyrone's antics were a fixture here, that he had a history with these men that went well beyond the sharing of old leather and common tasks.

Harry was surprised by this sudden shift in mood. With Resorts now in charge of things and all the money tied up in these fighters, he'd imagined a tighter operation, more of a military feel to the place, which was how it had seemed to him at first. But now he was seeing something else, more like a cross between a barroom and a playground. He didn't know what to make of it: whether Resorts allowed Ward a free hand in running things, or Tyrone, out of deference to his former glories, just got away with more. Either way, it was a welcome change, loose and easy and full of good feeling. But it confused him.

One by one, the boxers returned to their work, though Tyrone made no move to leave the ring. As Harry watched to see what would happen next, a tall skinny kid with an Afro and a Caesars T-shirt emerged at ringside, pulling on gloves. His name was Kenny—though Tyrone called him "Eel"—and he was maybe eighteen years old. A handler was with him, lacing the gloves and talking earnestly in his ear. Tyrone, who seemed to have expected his arrival, reached over the ropes and cuffed him lightly across the chest, which was as bony and dimensionless as a chicken's.

"Whattaya say, Eel? You gonna keep that right hand high, or am I gonna tap that skinny chin of yours till it falls off?" His humor had softened, serving a purpose now.

"He'll keep it up," said the handler, glancing up from the gloves with a hurried smile. "He'll keep it up, or I'll give you my personal permission to start jabbing like you meant it. Ain't that right, Kenny?"

"Do my best," was all the boy said, trying hard to smile, but too intent to manage it.

The handler then laced Tyrone's gloves, the headgear and mouth-pieces were fixed in place, and the two were through the ropes and into the ring. They touched gloves lightly, and the boy began to dance and Tyrone to shuffle. The boy threw a pair of early jabs, which Tyrone ducked as smoothly as lobbed grapefruits. Then he threw a third, harder this time, dropping his right in the process, and Tyrone answered with a left that caught the point of the boy's chin, though the impact was light and the boy seemed—or pretended—not to notice. Several more times this happened: a reaching jab, the right dropping as surely as an off-weighted seesaw. And each time Tyrone's left glove landed with a small *pop* on the boy's chin.

After the third or fourth time, there was a soft whistle from ringside. The boy, as intent as a veteran behind on points, heard nothing. Harry saw Tyrone glance over quickly, catch the handler's nod—and within seconds deliver a left that snapped the boy's head back like a branch in the wind. The right stayed higher after that, and Tyrone and the boy jabbed and circled for the remainder of two rounds. Toward the end of the second, the boy landed a solid left just forward of Tyrone's right ear, his first good connection. Tyrone backpedaled, grinned through his mouthpiece and raised his left glove-thumb in the air. The boy grinned back, his morning made.

***

"You with the paper, right? Sorry, mister, didn't mean to come up sudden."

An old man with ash-white hair, in a gray sweatshirt, had appeared next to Harry at ringside. The top of his head barely cleared Harry's shoulder. There was no doubting who he was.

"That's okay. Yes, I'm with *The Herald*. Harry Hopper. And you're Mr. Ward, right? You run this place?"

"Twenty-seven years. Not much longer, though. Getting way too old for this stuff."

But his eyes barely left the ring as he talked. He nodded in the direction of the boy, who had just landed his left and was circling Tyrone warily, every body part in motion.

"That kid's gonna be a fine boxer, got a big reach . . . So what you want with Tyrone?"

There was nothing friendly about the question—not the tone or the baldness or the way he kept his gaze fixed on the ring. Harry stayed silent for as long as he could manage, but it was clear the other man was awaiting an answer.

"I wanted to see him fight, is all. I heard he was a great fighter, a big addition to the gym. So I wanted to see him in action, maybe talk to him some. I hope that's not a problem."

"I don't know if that's a problem." The old man turned his head to face Harry now—only his head, and only barely. And he saw the anger in his half-squinted eyes. "But I know *you* a problem, mister."

"Because I want to talk to your fighter?"

"No, not because you want to talk to my fighter"—and here he swiveled to face Harry, his eyes meeting Harry's from close to a foot below. "And he ain't my fighter anyhow, he ain't *nobody's* fighter . . . It's 'cause anytime you talk to anybody, they come outta your typewriter looking like goons or jackasses or just poor dumb slobs. There ain't no poor slobs in my gym, mister, and if there was I wouldn't tell *you*."

"Look—"

"No, *you* look, Mister Harry Hopper. I read your write-ups in the paper, and I seen your picture and I know who you are. I seen you talking with Tyrone, and I know you come here looking to make some poor dumb nigger outta him—and I ain't gonna let you do it."

Harry was angry himself now, which made it hard to keep his voice steady. He told the other man he wasn't looking to make anybody into anything, and that whatever he might write about Tyrone would tell his story and not Harry's. But he was wasting both their time.

"Wouldn't matter what you wrote, mister. You see things *your* way, and it ain't the real way or the right way, and you ain't snooping for no trash in my gym."

Harry asked if he'd mind if he hung around for a while if he promised not to ask any questions.

"I never throw nobody outta my gym, 'less they start trouble. And when that happens usually I don't get there quick enough to do it myself."

The man turned and walked away, hands stuffed in his waistband. Harry stared after him until he disappeared behind the locker room door, then faced the ring again. Both fighters had removed their gloves by now. Tyrone, eyeing Harry from his stool in one corner, quickly looked away. It was as though somehow, by some secret signal, he had been banished.

Eight

———

The year of bliss ended abruptly on a Friday night in late September. Harry had had dinner with Anne, at a small Italian place on Route 30 an hour north of Atlantic City, near where she and Woody were staying for the weekend with friends. It was the early fall of 1985, more than five years since they'd split, and they had drifted by then, seamlessly enough, into their own construction of the divorced-parents' dance: Harry would drive north every third or fourth weekend to spend time with Woody; they'd come south every month or so as far as the Philadelphia suburbs to stay with an old college roommate of Anne's. Once in a while, like that night, the two of them would leave Woody with the roommate after his bedtime and go out somewhere for a meal. It was their way of honoring what both by now viewed as history—though for Harry at least, there was an overlay of sadness to every meeting. He had loved Anne, though the love by now had devolved into a sort of longing, rooted in the memory of what he sometimes feared he would never have again.

They parted outside the restaurant a little after ten. Harry would have liked to stay, but the bar had just shut down. It was chilly for early fall, and threatening rain. Watching Anne drive out of sight into the darkness, he felt suddenly, strangely, very alone, and unsure of almost everything.

He phoned Sarah from the booth outside. He didn't expect an answer (she was often not home on weekend nights before three in the morning, then would sleep past noon the next day), and was about to hang up when she answered. The voice on the other end was hers, but different, flat and faint. He asked if she was all right.

"I'm fine," she said, but so weakly he could almost not make out the words. He asked what was wrong.

"Nothing's wrong." But she sounded strange and faraway, as though the receiver was at a distance. He thought instantly of the bottle of pills she kept by her bed. She had told him they were for sleeping, but had once made a bad joke about taking too many.

She was crying now, sobbing quietly. He asked how many pills she'd taken.

"It doesn't matter," she said.

He said he'd be there in an hour. She was still crying when he hung up the phone.

The White Horse Pike picks up five minutes from where he was, and from there it was a straight shot south, most of the way through farmland and potato fields. Halfway down it began to rain in earnest. Harry was in the garage of Sarah's condo a few minutes after eleven, and at her door, six floors up, a minute later.

She was a mess, alternately crying and retching on the green living room couch, which was blotched now with phlegm and spilled gin or tequila, he couldn't tell which. Her hair was in mats, her eyes glazed and as red as a junkie's, mascara smeared from cheek to chin. Harry found a vial of Valium he'd never seen before overturned in the bathroom sink. It was very small, probably not large enough to kill her, he thought. He wondered if she'd thought that too.

He did all the things he thought he knew to do: made her vomit up whatever was left, then walked laps with her around the living room until her legs began working again. She didn't fight him, and she didn't say a word, just hung on limply like an oversized doll. Then he undressed her and put her in a lukewarm bath, where she sat, then half-lay, staring blankly at the chrome fixtures at her feet. The retching had stopped; the crying was more mournful now than anguished, and almost silent.

He sat on the closed toilet seat next to the bath, stroking her hair and adding hot water. Her nakedness, always before so wonderful, now seemed only sad.

"Why, Sarah?"

There was no answer the first time, only the blank stare and the quiet, mournful weeping. Then he asked again, "Why? Did you really want to die?"

Her head turned to him then, slowly, as though it were an effort.

"I don't know. Maybe." She said it so softly he had to strain to hear.

"Dying would be easier."

"Easier than *what?*"

"Oh, *Harry.*" She sighed weakly then turned her head away and stared again at the bath fixtures. The sadness in her eyes was ghostly.

"There's so much you don't know."

"So tell me."

Slowly, monotonously, over the next ten minutes, she recited for him—in flat, single sentences, with the water growing cool around her—the grotesqueries that made up her life. Touch of Class Escorts was run by a man named Lucchino, a soldier under Nicky Scarfo, by then the undisputed boss of the Philadelphia mob. Lucchino, known mostly by reputation for his crude mouth and fifty-inch waist, was her "manager" and sometime sexual user. While half of her work nights were spent on "blind calls" (like the ones when Harry had first met her at the Trump bar), the rest were "goodwill dates," arranged by Lucchino on orders from an underboss or *capo*, with men who did business with the mob: contractors, politicians, boxing promoters, freelance loan sharks. There were sometimes more than one at a time.

For the past two nights, she said, she'd been on a houseboat with a fight promoter—and part owner of Touch of Class—named Vic McGuigan, and two or three of his boxers. Harry knew of McGuigan; they called him the "Irish Don." Known to be connected to Scarfo, he had a hand in several businesses and had arranged some big-name fights at Resorts.

On her second night on the houseboat, she'd had sex with one of his boxers, who had forced her to do "disgusting things." She'd resisted, he'd hit her, called her filthy names, then turned her over to McGuigan, who had dangled her overboard by her ankles twenty miles from shore in the middle of the night. When they docked that morning, the boxer had complained to Lucchino, who had slapped her across the room and told her she was "scumbag property" for any man he wanted her to see. Then he had used her and sent her home.

"He's like the devil," Sarah said. "They all are. And McGuigan is the worst." There was no escaping them, except death, she said, and there were times she thought that death would be better.

After the first few minutes, Harry heard without listening. He felt like two people: the one there on that toilet top, hearing this tortured person whose beauty and poise he had compared in his mind to a diva's, telling him she wanted to be dead for reasons so grotesque he could barely conjure them; the other afloat, detached, observing, a butterfly collecting data.

"Jesus, Sarah, how can you do it? How can you fuck that guy?"

It was the wrong thing to say. He knew it, and regretted it instantly. But at that moment it was all he could think of or see: Sal Lucchino, his jelly-flesh belly rolling like a water balloon on top of her. It was beyond understanding for him.

"I don't fuck *him*, Harry. He fucks *me*."

She glared at him stonily from the tub, her eyes like little beads. It was the first thing she'd said with any inflection at all.

"You don't get it, do you? This apartment *belongs* to McGuigan. It's his place, his furniture." She gestured at her soiled dress on the tile floor—"his clothes. Everything I have is his. *I hate him. I hate them all. I hate them so much.*"

"I'm sorry," Harry said. "I shouldn't have said that." But Sarah only shivered and stared at the water. He gave her a towel and helped her out of the bathtub, then put her to bed. There were no more words between them that night.

***

But now he was scared. No one in Atlantic City in those days wasn't scared of Nicky Scarfo, and of anyone connected to him. The police feared him, his underbosses feared him (he had murdered at least two of them), the press feared him, his own family feared him.

No one knew for sure how many people he had killed, or ordered killed—beginning with the longshoreman he'd stabbed to death in 1963 in an argument over a diner's booth. Since the spring of 1980, when the hit on Angelo Bruno had set off a war for mob control, the killings hadn't stopped: Bruno's killer, "Tony Bananas" Caponigro, shot less than a month later, his anus stuffed with $20 bills (Sicilian for excessive greed), found in a car trunk in the south Bronx; then "Big John" McCullough, Al Salerno, Frank Simone, Frank Stillitano, Phil "Chicken Man" Testa—followed by Testa's twenty-eight-year-old son, both dead of gunshot wounds and left at the side of a road. And no one knew how many small-time pimps, bookies, meth dealers and loan sharks who'd balked at paying protection money or had otherwise made trouble.

It took nothing for Scarfo to order a hit. He controlled the Atlantic City rackets (and would until the Feds put him away three years later on a fifty-five-year sentence for racketeering and murder) with an efficiency that relied almost solely on fear. No one dared cross him. Harry knew there'd be no deliverance for a hooker who got out of line.

For weeks that followed, he would be haunted by nightmarish images—and several times actual nightmares—of Sarah disappearing, vanished from the earth, her lovely body crumpled in a car trunk or forty feet down in Absecon Bay. He thought of her the night before, hanging by her ankles over dark water at the mercy of a drunken sleaze, and knew without a doubt that if he'd dropped her over the side they'd have shrugged it off as a business loss.

He thought of other things too that night, watching Sarah sleep in the darkness of her bedroom. He thought of his mother, twenty-five years before, deciding to end her life with sleeping pills at the age of thirty-eight, with her eight-year-old son in the next room and her husband across town with another woman. He thought of how lost and alone she must have felt when she did it, of what it must be like to feel that lost, to not understand how you got there or how to find your way back.

He sat there all night thinking these thoughts, on the edge of that queen-sized bed, until long after a gray dawn overtook the darkness in the room. While Sarah, the tightness in her face at last released, slept soundlessly next to him under the flowered quilt that belonged to the man who pimped out her body to boxers on houseboats.

Nine

———

Sarah was still asleep, and hadn't moved in hours, when Harry left her condo that Saturday morning. He thought she'd probably sleep all day. But he couldn't stay another minute. Everything there felt weighted with gloom.

He traded his dress shirt for a Memories sweatshirt of Sarah's (a gift from The Geator, she'd told him), found an old Phillies cap, and went out to run. It was raining hard, with a wind blowing in from the ocean. The sky was the color of ashes. But it felt glorious to be outside.

He ran east to the Boardwalk, then stayed on it all the way through Ventnor—Atlantic City's southern neighbor, the second of four beach-front towns that succeed one another like fenceposts on the seven-mile island they share—until the boards ended and the dunes began. Then, because he couldn't think of anything better to do and because the rain on his face and the pain in his gut felt almost like a balm, he kept running: south along Atlantic Avenue through the gold coast of Margate, whose faux Tudor mansions, once the summer homes of Philadelphia's rich, were now the year-round addresses of local CEOs, mob *capos* and casino shift bosses.

***

Before there were mansions, or Ventnor or Margate or Atlantic City or the island they sit on, there were three long, skinny sandbars, each roughly three miles in length and a few hundred yards wide which, over time, filled in to form one. The Lenni Lenape people called it Absegami, or Little Water. The first white men to come were probably New England whalers in the mid-18th century, who used its wide beaches to gut and skin their catches, leaving behind the huge, bleached skeletons that would be found by the clammers, oystermen and farmers who came after.

At some point in the early 1800s, the island was discovered by mainland day-trippers who would row out for picnics on summer afternoons. One of them was a South Jersey doctor, Jonathan Pitney—to be known as the "father of Atlantic City"—who sold investors on the idea of developing the north end of the island ("Further Island" at the time) as a health resort for the wealthy. This led to the first railroad, in 1854, followed by food stands and bathhouses, then small guesthouses, shops and arcades. And by the early 1870s, the grand hotels and Boardwalk that would define the resort for a century after.

By 1880, as depicted in *Harper's Weekly*, life there was positively idyllic:

Its streets and avenues are broad and straight, planted with great numbers of shade trees . . . In front of them, offering an unobstructed, limitless expanse of ocean stretching away to the far horizon, is the Boardwalk . . . This is the promenade, the center of life and interest; everybody strolls over the two miles of Boardwalk in search of exercise and amusement . . . [or] for a few breaths of the very purest and freshest ocean air.

The early years were a non-stop frolic: Vaudeville, opera, minstrel shows, theater, beer gardens, ballroom dancing, carnival rides, fireworks, snake charmers, palm readers, jugglers, flagpole sitters, high-wire walkers, a diving horse, a boxing kangaroo. In 1881, a ninety-ton, six-story, wood-and-tin elephant—Lucy—was built to promote real estate sales.

The rich arrived in private railway cars, met at the station by uniformed valets driving four-horse coaches. Once at their hotels—The Traymore, The Ritz, The Marlborough-Blenheim, The Breakers, The Chalfonte–Haddon Hall—they would sit under palm fronds in carpeted pavilions and sip gin fizzes to a background of string quartets.

Those were the glory years. "The gentle years," one city historian would say of them later. There was always a seedier side, of course—gambling rooms, brothels, opium dens—but through at least the first three or four decades it was still, at least mostly, about fun.

The rot set in slowly. The first sign may have been as early as 1890, when the Philadelphia *Bulletin* published the addresses of twenty-four "pestilential" brothels. By 1911, and the report that a quarter of the names on the county voting list were fictitious, corruption had become endemic. Two years after that, Louis Kuehnle, the first of a fifty-year dynasty of bosses who ran the city like a personal fiefdom—extorting every gambling room and brothel, ferrying Black voters between polling places on election day at $2 a vote—went to prison.

But the times were good, and no one paid much attention. Kuehnle would serve six months, and be greeted by a brass band on his return. "They'll build a monument to me someday," he predicted. ("They never did," Harry would write in a column seventy-five years later. "But I've heard there's a Kuehnle Avenue out by the wastewater plant.")

Then came Prohibition—Atlantic City's zenith. By 1923, a fleet of thirty ships a day were running bootleg whiskey from Canada's coastal islands to the beaches of Absecon Island—by one count, more than a third of all the illegal liquor smuggled into the U.S. Speakeasies catered on weekends to standing-room crowds; make-shift casinos, from grocery-store punchboards to felt-tabled baccarat parlors, flourished alongside. In May of 1929, the first-ever Mafia "conference"—Al Capone, Lucky Luciano, Bugsy Siegel, Meyer Lansky and any other early-century mob chief you could name—took over the Ritz and the Breakers for a weekend to smooth out problems and divvy up the rackets. The resort by then had a thousand hotels and rooming houses, twenty-one theaters, ninety-nine daily trains and three airports. Its 1930 population was 66,000. It could accommodate 400,000 guests a night. It was The Playground of The Nation, The Resort For Everyone.

Then came the Depression. Then the end of Prohibition. Then the war. Almost overnight, the city went to its knees. Unable to meet payroll in 1933, it began paying its employees in scrip. By 1939, the real estate base had sunk by a third and the tax rate had more than doubled. In 1941, Nucky Johnson, the mightiest boss of them all, with his red lapel carnation and Pierce Arrow limousine, went to federal prison for tax evasion—his income from vice alone had exceeded a half-million dollars a year.

A year later, the resort was taken over by the military, transformed within weeks to a wartime training base known locally as Camp Boardwalk. Its hotels were stripped down to become barracks; the Chalfonte–Haddon Hall and the Traymore were now the Thomas M. England Hospital for neurosurgery and limb amputations. Over the next four years, 300,000 soldiers would train on its boardwalk and beach.

In 1945, the war ended. The city, a resort once again, resumed its slow death. In the 1950s, with the coming of low-cost jet travel and the interstate highway system, the rich and middle class began passing it by for newer playgrounds—Florida, Las Vegas, the Caribbean—leaving Atlantic City to what one local paper would call the "lower element," with their box lunches and two-dollar gas budgets. The population declined by a quarter, then by nearly a half; the grand hotels were rehabbed as nursing homes or budget apartments. By 1975, it was among the poorest cities in the east.

Casinos were to be the savior. Packaged as a "noble experiment" that would lead the resort into a "new renaissance" and funded by a million-dollar ad campaign, the 1976 state-wide referendum ended on Election Night 1976 in what Harry, still at his post at the Hartford paper, would later call "an orgy of free liquor and impossible dreams"— some of which, even at that early date, were his own.

It had been "a glorious century in a quintessentially American city," he wrote of the resort's history for his Connecticut readers. "It was a time of providence, sin, greed and grandeur, of genius and trickery, outlaws and titans. All built around promises as flimsy as gauze."

***

He ran until he reached the wood-and-tin–sculpted Lucy, still thriving a hundred years after her birth. "The only elephant on earth you can walk through and come out alive," they told the tourists who had come for years by the thousands to climb through her. The only tourists he saw that morning were a couple in their sixties, hunched under a single umbrella, banging on the closed door of a blue tour bus parked at the curb, whose driver sat at the wheel sipping coffee. Harry watched them for a minute. Then, too spent to run another yard and soaked through with rain and sweat, he turned around and began the walk back.

Everything felt different now. Everything felt caved-in. Sarah, until the night before the source of a kind of careless amazement, now seemed to him a frightened but precious child, hopelessly entrapped. He couldn't imagine what rescue there could be.

***

He was gone nearly two hours. When he arrived back, he thought for a second he might be at the wrong door—the woman who greeted him wore a green terrycloth robe he'd never seen, almost to her feet, which were bare. She wore no makeup, no lipstick. Her hair, slicked back from her face and still damp from washing, shone like new metal. She looked gorgeous, but not in any way he knew. She looked like a wife.

"God, you're soaked through," she said on seeing him. "You must be freezing."

They were both standing just inside the door, Sarah in her strange new bathrobe, Harry shivering and dripping wet.

"You look different," he said, still half-stupefied by the change.

"I cleaned up. I had to get rid of last night."

"How are you feeling?"

"Much better, really . . . I'm sorry I was such a mess."

"You scared me, you know? You really scared me."

"I know. I said I'm sorry. I'll say it again if you want." Her voice was crisp and careful.

He hugged her. She hugged him back, but not with much feeling, he thought.

He changed clothes and toweled off his wet hair. The bathroom was pristine, no sign of the debacle of the night before.

"So what's going on?" he said, now on the couch next to Sarah. It was more an opener than a question.

She sat stiffly, looking straight ahead.

"I can't keep seeing you, Harry."

Harry said nothing. He'd had the same thought himself, persistently, through most of the past eight or ten hours, but had pushed it away each time and didn't want to hear it now.

"It's not good. They hurt people. They don't care who they hurt."

"So they'll hurt *you?*"

"Not if I keep doing what they want."

"Why now? Is this because of what happened on that boat?"

"Maybe. I don't know. What happened out there scared me a lot. But things are different now, too."

"Different how?"

She paused here, and dropped her eyes. "I'm Sal's main girl now. The 'top horse in his stable'—that's what he calls me." She gave a twisted little smile here, as though in embarrassment or apology.

"The clients, a lot of them, are big people. One last week was a casino owner, another was a big political guy. The boxer on the boat was some kind of champion or something. Don't ask me their names, 'cause I usually don't know and I wouldn't tell you anyway. But he watches me like a hawk now, all the time."

"How long has it been like this?"

"It's been happening for a while. The last couple weeks especially. Sal calls it a 'promotion.' And I get paid more now for my dates."

"So how much are we talking about? How much does it take to *buy your life?*"

It was a hateful thing to say. But he was angry now. Angry at Sarah, at the men who ran her life, at the grotesque unfairness of it all. And at his own impotence. Especially that.

"Do you really want to know, Harry? Is that really what you want to talk about?"

"No. I hate talking about it, actually. I just need to understand."

She looked at him for a long moment without speaking, then sighed deeply and answered, as flatly as though reciting from a rate sheet.

"I get three hundred an hour, two thousand for the night. When there's a convention, it'll be four, five grand for the weekend. I keep a quarter. Plus tips."

Harry's mind swung between images: the beautiful mob-connected hooker sleeping with mayors and casino bosses for thousands of dollars a night; and this frightened, damaged but dazzling woman, so like a child sometimes, who had been his lover for more than a year and whom he was coming to love now more by the minute. He didn't know how he could hold the two together in his head, or even if he wanted to.

Her eyes were closed now, her hands steepled over her mouth and nose as though in prayer. Harry could hear her slow breaths. When she spoke again it was almost a whisper.

"You're a reporter. They *hate* reporters, they hate them almost as much as cops. If they found out, they could hurt you. Or me. And I'm not supposed to see anyone anyway. Except for the johns."

"How would they know?"

"I told you, Sal knows every move I make. I have to call in every time I get to a place, and again when I leave. Even when I'm not going out, I'm supposed to be by the phone."

Harry had feared this moment would come. Now it was here, and he felt desperate to somehow not let it happen.

"How about if I was just like a regular john? If I see you at hotels, pay you the hourly rate?"

Sarah shook her head tiredly. "I don't want to take money from you. And you can't afford that anyway."

But she was too worn out to fight, and in the end that was how they left it. They would meet only at hotels in the city and no more often than twice a month. Harry would book the rooms under a false name, and always pay in cash (though Sarah would "help out"). There would be no calls between meetings—Sarah was convinced Sal had a trace on her phone—and Harry would contact her only through Touch of Class.

There would be no more nights at Memories, or beaches or movies or amusement parks or dinners out. Only hotel rooms and fake names and dollars changing hands. The meagerness of it all was almost too much to bear.

"I'm sorry, Harry," Sarah said wearily once the plan was in place.

Harry asked her, as he had more than once before, if she had any plan for getting away, for having her own life once all this was over. Her answer was as bankrupt as ever.

"I don't know what's in the future for me. Just that it'll be far away from here. You have to trust me on that."

He didn't trust her, of course. But there was nothing he could say. He ached already for the hole her absence would leave. Yet to tell her so then would have weighted the moment past its limits, and maybe forced an answer he couldn't have borne. And so he kept silent.

"Are you sure this, this hotel thing—this is really what you want?" Sarah asked him toward the end.

"It's not even close to what I want," Harry said. "But it'll keep you in my life."

It was still raining when he left her condo that Saturday. It would rain through the night and most of the next day. Harry sat home, drinking tequila mix from a can and watching the Yankees lose to the Red Sox on TV.

Ten

___

It was nearly a month before he saw Tyrone again, at the gym on a Sunday morning in mid-October—Sunday being Toby's day off. Most of the same faces were there; the kid named Eel was sparring in the ring with a boxer Harry had seen before, who looked old enough to be his father. But there were no handlers in sight, only fighters. Harry found Tyrone at the weight bench, spotting for another man. He figured Ward had warned him to keep his distance, and was expecting resistance. But there was none, or none that he could see.

"Hey man, ain't seen you in a while. What's doing with you?"

Harry told him he'd come hoping to see him fight again, and that he'd brought a camera this time. The camera was mostly an excuse for being there, though he had been known to take his own photos occasionally if he wanted to pitch some story to Alcorn but thought it might be a hard sell.

"Sure. You come at the right time. I be going a couple rounds with DeWayne here"—he gestured toward the older man in the ring with Eel—"then maybe with this dude we call Owl, if he ever shows up . . .

And I got some of my own photos too, in case you be wanting to see them. Ones they took of me back a ways, when I was fighting."

Harry felt encouraged. Tyrone was a man naturally given to trust. There seemed to be no artifice about him at all, and very little of the natural defenses most of us carry around like second skins. As sad as this might have been for Tyrone, given all the betrayals it seemed he had suffered, it made him easy to work with. And impossible not to like.

Within a few minutes Eel and the boxer named DeWayne wound up their last round of sparring. Eel climbed out of the ring and began unlacing his gloves, while the older man remained, pulled a stool through the ropes from ringside and sat down, his gloves still on, breathing in long breaths through his nose.

"DeWayne, he run outta gas his last bout," Tyrone said, nodding toward DeWayne, who nodded back weakly from his stool. "Run out about two rounds too soon—would've won otherwise. We gotta build up his wind, make sure that don't happen no more."

A minute later the two were in the ring together, trading jabs. Tyrone was a different fighter than he'd been with Eel the month before: shiftier, lighter on his feet, more stick-and-move. But there was an economy to it, too—no waste, no flash or hustle. Dewayne was plainly a veteran, cagey but careful, holding to the center of the ring. But he was no match for Tyrone, who measured him with every move, landing two punches for every one he took, mostly jabs and crosses. His right was more feinted than used, the restraint as explicit as the talent.

Tyrone was thirty-three years old and hadn't had a money fight in three years. But from what Harry could see and what he recalled from the films he had watched he hadn't lost a thing. His belly was as flat and hard as a fighter ten years younger; his hands were as quick as they'd ever been. He was a smarter fighter than he'd seemed in the films: he danced less, shuffled more, and waited for opponents now rather than trying to out-jazz them.

Untested for three years and lacking any management but his own, boxing with headgear and heavy padded gloves in a ring lit by fluorescent tubing and smelling of ammonia, he had become a veteran in the gym. And learned to box for the love of it.

The longer Harry watched him, the more he thought of Sarah on the dance floor. The same easy grace, the same power to step across limits. You saw it sometimes in the very best performers: gymnasts, skiers, tennis players, musicians. But to describe it is impossible. Harry was reminded of the passage from *Death in the Afternoon*, where the young writer tries to explain to the old lady in the Madrid café the artistry of the matador's pass and kill. The explanation is a failure, as it was bound to be—there being no explaining transcendence.

The kid named Owl never showed up. From time to time Harry scanned the floor, looking for any sign of Ward, who he'd heard sometimes came in on off-days. But it seemed he'd stayed home that Sunday.

Then, late in the morning, with Tyrone working the speed bag, he saw two boxers he didn't recognize arrive with an older man—the first white man Harry had seen at the gym—who appeared to be their manager. Tyrone looked over and seemed to stiffen, his face now with a sudden resoluteness.

"I'm done here," he said, flipped off his bag gloves and tossed them on a shelf. Harry asked what was the problem.

"Somebody I don't want to see." But he just shook his head when Harry asked who it was.

***

It was a little past noon. Harry offered to buy him a burger at The Lighthouse Pub, a block down the street from the gym. Tyrone was quiet for several moments and Harry thought perhaps he hadn't heard him. Then his face loosened its tightness and there was the beginnings of that grin.

"How about *two* burgers?" he said.

He ordered them both extra rare, with a side order of fries and another of chicken wings. Harry ordered a pitcher of beer for them to share. "Haven't eaten since yesterday," Tyrone announced between bites. It was all Harry heard from him till he was midway through the second burger.

After that, though, they covered some ground. Tyrone had been born in the Inlet, which he hadn't left till he shipped out in '71 to Vietnam, where he'd lost a brother and cousin but won a Bronze Star in Quang Tri on his nineteenth birthday. He was close to his mother, who lived three blocks away and worked as a housekeeper at The Tropicana, but barely remembered his father, who'd been gone since he was five. He had three still-living brothers he almost never saw, and a disabled younger sister he said he "loved a lot," who lived in town with their mother.

He had started boxing at six, he said, when an older brother had taken him to Toby's one day after school:

"And Toby, who I don't even know who he is, he hands me this itty-bitty pair of gloves, ties them on, gets down on his knees and starts pretend-boxing with me. He shows me how to throw a jab, I do this little tap thing on his chin, and next thing I know he falls over like he's dead. That was crazy, man. I think I was back the next day."

He said that he loved boxing "more than anything except loving"— and grinned like a schoolboy when he said it—and that "except for the money part of things," he was happier at The Lucky Lady than he'd been fighting at the casino showrooms.

"Toby, he run the place like he always did, no different from before. Don't matter who own it now, there still a lotta love there, like you probably seen. Ain't no love in the casinos, just a lot of mean shit going down."

Harry asked if it was true what the paper had said, that he and the others thought of Toby as something like a father. The answer came quickly.

"Sure I do, man. Exactly like that. He been there since I was a little kid. Been good to my mama, to my brothers, gave me money sometimes, helped me out when I come back from 'Nam. Helped me out through all this last stuff, too . . .

"So yeah, exactly like a father. I never had no real one anyways, so it's not like I got somebody to compare him to."

Harry thought he'd waited long enough to ask again about the man he'd seen in the gym.

"I was wonderin' when you was gonna get around to that. His name's Ruben Florio. He used to manage me."

"What happened?"

"Shit happened, is what happened. He the guy that sold me out. The guy that told me to throw that fight. He the reason I ain't fighting no more."

Over the next few minutes, between mouthfuls of chicken wings and french fries, he described to Harry—following his promise not to write a word of it—how Florio, whom he said he'd trusted "like a number-two father," had told him, half an hour before his last fight, in February of '82, that "it would be better" if he lost. He said that it hadn't been his idea, but that losing would help him more in the long run than winning would, and that his next fight—assuming he lost that one—would be in Philadelphia against a ranked middleweight named Peaches Johnson, which would be a good payday and a step up toward a higher ranking.

He had told Tyrone he didn't have to go down if he didn't want, that all he had to do was throw fewer punches and stay away from using his right, and the rest would take care of itself. Ruben had promised to advise him further between rounds, and asked that he trust him, since he had his best interests at heart and would never do anything to hurt his career.

"He wanted me to believe that, man, wanted me to trust him—that it would be '*better if I lost*,' that's how he said it to me."

His voice was louder now, and angrier, his hands gripping the sides of the tabletop as though to hold himself down.

"Shit, man, I didn't know *what* to believe, didn't have time to think about what he said or what I was going to do, or nothin'. I didn't decide to lose, I didn't decide not to lose, I didn't decide *nothin'*."

Ruben had talked to him between rounds, he said, and he had nodded his head without listening, and before he knew it the fight was over and he had won. There hadn't been much hitting on either side, and the crowd had booed toward the end.

"They booed me, man, they fuckin' booed me, I never been booed in my life!"

After the result was announced—the decision was close on all three cards, but it was unanimous—Ruben told him he'd made a big mistake and would be lucky to ever fight again.

"Then the next day, I show up at the gym and he tells me he's sorry. He's *so sorry*, he couldn't be more fuckin' sorry, like I was supposed to feel for him or something—but that he can't be my manager no more. I want to know why, and he just say, 'You shoulda lost like I told you.' Then he tells me again how sorry he is and how it wasn't his idea."

This was a different Tyrone than the one Harry had thought he was starting to know. He saw now the bitterness that lay behind the trash-talking, grin-a-minute front he wore around the gym. He saw the depth of the betrayal he'd suffered. And in the process, the boxer's anger—or a piece of it—was becoming his own.

In the end, Tyrone said, it was Toby who had told him what happened.

"He always the one to tell me the bad stuff. He the one told me when my uncle died, he called me in 'Nam after my brother got killed. So it figured I'd hear it from him. There's gotta be a bunch of other trainers and all who knew what was going down, but he the only one who give it to me straight."

The fighter he'd beaten, Esteban Castillo, Toby had told him, was owned by a group of backers who had wanted big things for him. He had fought only five bouts, had lost one of them, and needed a win over a ranked fighter to draw some notice from the promoters. Tyrone was to have been that win.

One of Castillo's backers had approached Vic McGuigan, the local promoter, who had promised to arrange things. McGuigan had talked to Ruben Florio, who had talked to Tyrone, and that was where things had stood.

Harry knew the name right away: McGuigan, the promoter on the houseboat, the man in the vision he still kept seeing, of Sarah upside down over black water. The sudden rage he felt at this new knowledge, the sense of the hateful connectivity of things—of Tyrone, like Sarah, being fed like lumps of coal into this furnace of greed and deceit—would grow from that moment, until it would become too much to contain.

Toby's advice to him, Tyrone said, was that he get out of town, go someplace else—to Philadelphia or New York—and start again. He'd never get another fight in Atlantic City as long as McGuigan was arranging them. And no local manager would risk taking him on.

"What Toby said was, Atlantic City's the dirtiest place in America for boxing, even just for living, ever since casinos came here. And that I'd be lucky to get out. He even gave me some money, offered to help me get started someplace else."

And Tyrone had tried. For more than three months he had bounced around the gyms in Philadelphia doing odd jobs, sparring anyone close to his weight class, looking for a trainer or manager to work with. He'd had two offers, he said, neither one worth considering.

And he was homesick. He missed his mother and sister, and Toby and The Lucky Lady. So in the end he just gave up and came home. Within a week he was delivering flowers.

"The guys at the gym—they my homies, man. We go back. I know some of 'em since I was, like, two years old. And the young kids coming up, like Eel, I like a big brother to them. The gym's like my world, man. Ain't no place else I want to be."

Eleven

———

In Atlantic City meanwhile, the rot was spreading like a virus. It was the late fall of 1985; there were nine casinos now, grossing $2 billion a year. But the numbers were far short of forecasts and had only just begun their decline. Unemployment in the county was twice the national rate, crime in the city had doubled; you couldn't drive a block on Pacific Avenue at night without being hustled. The last mayor was in federal prison on charges of extortion. One casino president had been stripped of his post for underworld ties, another for bribery.

The mob wars, and killings, showed no signs of abating. One of the latest had been twenty-eight-year-old Salvatore Testa, knighted by *The Herald* newsroom as the Scarfo family's "fastest rising star," who was found wrapped in a blanket by the side of a road in Gloucester Township, a bullet hole behind each ear. (The reporter who'd written the story phoned Alcorn at home, drunk, the night the body was found—"I think I signed that kid's death warrant"—then didn't come to work for a week.) Five days later, Testa's newest recruit, twenty-two-year-old Michael Micali, was found dead a mile from his boss's body, also shot twice in the head.

Duffy had taken Alcorn's advice and peddled his story of Donald Trump's mob dealings to the only other paper in the region, a scrappy investigative weekly, *The Sun*, which had promised to publish it. The story had grown in the meantime: In addition to the casino plots Trump had bought from mob operators, he had bought an Atlantic City night-club, Le Bistro, for $1.1 million—in a third-party deal using his lawyer's secretary as signee—from Sal Testa, two years before Testa wound up in that blanket by the side of the road. Several years earlier, his political donations in New York had been cited by that city's organized-crime task force. And there was an account of a high-rolling member of the Russian mafia Trump had hosted at his casino and on his yacht—all of it falling under the general heading of what Duffy called "questionable or outright illegal dealings with mafia-affiliated firms or individuals."

The front-page story, well-sourced and carefully written, had run in *The Sun* in late April of 1985. A little more than a month later, at three in the morning of June 1st, two magnum-sized whiskey bottles fused with gasoline-soaked rag strips were thrown through the weekly's front window. No culprit was named or arrested. The paper burned to the ground.

***

For Harry, this daily churn of filth and corruption and everyday misery, which had once drawn him like a beacon, now seemed only toxic. He woke up nearly every day depressed. He despaired for Tyrone. He couldn't drive down Pacific Avenue at night or read about another mob hit without being consumed anew with worries for Sarah.

On an afternoon in late October, having waited more than the two weeks they'd agreed on, he called Touch of Class from his desk at *The Herald* and asked to book an hour with "Dawn." The woman on the line promised cheerily to have her call back. He waited at his desk till after dark for her call, which never came. He tried again the next day, and again two days later, with the same result each time. "I gave her your message, she'll call back when she can," the woman told him the last time he called, no longer so cheery. He promised himself he wouldn't try again. And for many months, he wouldn't.

But he missed her. He missed her more than he had ever missed anyone. Often, late at night when he couldn't sleep or had had too much to drink, he'd drive downbeach through Ventnor and look up at her windows in the condo, which were nearly always dark. And he'd almost convince himself that they'd done something horrible to her, or that she'd taken her life and was lying up there alone and rotting in her bed. And he'd be wretched all the next day. Then the next night or the one after, there'd be a light on, and he could almost feel his heart jump. And the cycle would begin again.

***

One day in late November, Alcorn approached him with a new assignment, about an aging mobster named Harry "The Hunchback" Riccobene and his (failed) attempt to unseat Nicky Scarfo. For the first time in his nearly six years at the paper, Harry balked. He was feeling burned out on mob stories, he told his boss—he'd written dozens by then, many of them pretty grisly. Could he "maybe take a break," at least for a time? He was surprised by how quickly Alcorn agreed.

"Give you time to write more of the longer stuff. You're probably better at that anyway."

Harry said he wasn't sure how to take that.

"Take it as a compliment," Alcorn said. "You're good at the grab-you-in-the-gut stuff, the welfare moms, the train-wreck lives, all that kinda shit."

It happened slowly at first. But by the end of that winter Harry had a whole new beat: all feature stories, all the time, many of them portraits of what he came to refer to as the "underside people"—day trippers, busted gamblers, squeegee people, evicted tenants, old-timers in the Inlet who remembered the glory days. In January he spent a whole afternoon with an eighty-five-year-old Black man who lived in the same Inlet tenement he'd been born in; he'd worked forty years as a bellman and bootblack at the old Traymore ("The swankiest place on the 'Walk in its day, God bless it"), and became close to some of its regulars—notably his favorite, Cornelius Vanderbilt IV, "a gentleman like there never was"—who had sometimes gifted him with their discarded suits and shoes. His two-room flat was piled with them; he hobbled around the Inlet all day in decades-old double-breasted tweeds, shiny two-tone oxfords, and felt fedoras or porkpie hats he traded off every few hours. He went by the name—the only name anyone knew him by—of Cornelius Vanderbilt Massey.

Harry's star rose quickly. In the spring of '86 he was given a column—christened "Changing Times"—which would run weekly, on any subject he chose, so long as it related to the general theme of change (positive or not) within the region.

For the first several weeks, he stayed mostly with portraits of the Inlet poor, living in gutted wood tenements in the shadows of $400-a-night hotel suites. Later, he focused on the inequities of a state system that allowed casinos to allocate millions in escrowed "reinvestment" money to the refurbishment of their lobbies while street hoods hawked cocaine in vacant buildings a hundred yards away and homeless Black mothers with infant kids lived in flophouse motels at the city's expense. From time to time, he devoted a column to a local philanthropist or soup-kitchen do-gooder, but most times his focus was the underside.

One of his early columns was a 400-word portrait of The Lucky Lady, which Harry called "the gym of old leather and young dreams." He wrote about the hopes it offered to kids from the Inlet like Tyrone,

Eel and the older DeWayne, each of whom told his story to Harry over the burgers he bought them at The Lighthouse Pub.

Tyrone had been quieter that day than before. His mother was in the hospital, he said, with "long-time diabetes, and now some kinda cancer, which they just this year discovered." He said that he visited every day, but that she was often too sleepy from the treatments to know he was there, and that now with the diabetes, they were "talking about taking off half her leg."

Harry said he was sorry, and offered to drive him to the hospital anytime he needed. Tyrone thanked him, but said that Toby usually took him for those trips.

"Maybe just pray," he said. "I don't know what else there be. She been a good mama to me a whole long time. I sure don't want to see her go."

There was no mention that day of Ruben Florio and the career-ending fight—which, though certainly believable, would be near impossible to prove. Harry told Tyrone he planned to come back again soon: "And maybe next time, if things are better with your mom, we could talk some more about boxing." Tyrone nodded, though Harry wasn't sure he'd really heard him.

***

The months passed. By the fall of '86, "Changing Times" was being touted by civic groups as "the conscience of the city." Alcorn dubbed Harry "the Boardwalk Breslin"; to a Philadelphia talk-show host he was "Atlantic City's Bob Dylan, melting hearts with his notepad and phone." For the first time in a long time, Harry was coming to feel he might have a role to play in just how much of a Sodom the city was destined to be.

Meanwhile he continued to work at being a father. It was harder than before. Woody had turned eight the winter before; his life was widening—soccer and hockey, birthdays, pool parties and overnights. The back-and-forth, every-other-weekend plan had died a slow death, as it was bound to: Harry was driving north now every second weekend, Woody hadn't been south since the summer.

Their routine rarely varied. Harry would arrive, more or less on time, at whatever practice or scrimmage was scheduled that Saturday—Woody played Mite-League soccer for the Raiders, Peewee hockey for the Kings—make small talk on the sidelines with any parents who still remembered him, then take his son for lunch at The Four Aces Alehouse, an out-of-time place with varnished wood tables, connect-the-dots placemats and overweight waitresses who would coo over Woody like a troupe of grandmothers. Woody would order a cheese-burger and Coke, Harry a sub and a beer; Woody would connect the dots on his own placemat, then start working his way through Harry's. Their exchanges were as scripted as their meals:

"You're getting really good on those skates."

"I guess."

"And with your stick, too. That was a terrific shot you took there at the end."

"It's what we practice."

"How're things at school?"

"About the same."

"So what do you think about a movie tonight?"

"Okay, I guess."

In the spring and summer they'd gone sometimes to baseball games—Hartford had a double-A team that Woody followed. In the winter it was mostly bowling or the movies, often both. Then they'd return for an early supper with Anne, who had probably made a pot roast or spaghetti and a salad. They would sit around the small kitchen table, ladling out the food to each other, passing a pitcher of iced tea back and forth. Woody's remoteness would have dropped away like a cloud: he talked now of wrist-shots, video games, a class geography project. The three of them would laugh and tell stories; it was almost like being a family again. Which to Harry was the saddest part of it all.

Sometime later, with Woody in bed upstairs, he and Anne would sit a while at opposite ends of the living room couch, share a bottle of wine and talk about their lives, and their son's. On one of those evenings, in the early fall, Harry told her of the distance he felt from his son.

"He's almost like a stranger. I can't figure out how to break through."

"Just let him know you're there for him, that's all you can do. He's confused, Harry. He's afraid to let himself feel close to you, then not see you again for two weeks. Think how tough that's gotta be for an eight-year-old."

"I *have* thought of it. I've also thought of how tough it's gotta be for an eight-year-old to feel he has to choose between dads."

This was a reference to the man Anne was seeing, an architect named Richard, the ex-husband of a mutual friend, who was teaching Woody to fly-fish and went bicycling with him on weekends. But while Harry did worry sometimes about his son's torn allegiance, he knew this probably wasn't the real issue. And he knew it was a stupid thing to say.

"Woody only has one dad, and he knows it. And there's no choosing involved. You know that, Harry."

It was so Anne—ever reasonable, ever calm—which left him, every time, feeling alone on some island of idiocy with nothing smart or even sensible to say.

But the next thing she said he wasn't remotely ready for. It came out sounding almost breezy, or like an afterthought. Or a well-rehearsed delivery.

"I'm glad you mentioned Richard, though. We're going to be married next spring. It'll be a small thing, probably right here at the house. We haven't picked a date yet, but we'd like you to be there."

They would be married six months later. Harry would be there, and would propose a toast to them both. But at the moment all he felt was bereft.

***

Sometimes on weeknights after work with nothing else to do, Harry would find himself at the blackjack tables, these days usually at Caesars or Bally's. He'd hardly been at all in the past two years, and playing now seemed somehow to reconnect him with that small, simpler part of himself. He was a more than decent player and enjoyed the fast pace of the game. Two or three times during those months, he had wins of $400 or so, which was always good for a reprieve from the bouts of dark thinking he so often sank into. Just as often he lost.

Occasionally he saw women. First it was a younger reporter from the paper he'd liked from a distance for a while. On their second or third date they went back to her place after dinner and had what passed for sex, but everything about it was awkward and a disappointment—to them both, Harry guessed—after which they returned almost seamlessly to being the mutually fond colleagues they'd been.

Another was the ex-wife of a casino vice president, Nancy Donnelly, who had been a source for a column Harry had written about local charities. They dated off and on for several weeks—she was smart and pretty and good-hearted, and they shared some snippets of their histories—before she told him, in a charged confession late one night, that she'd been sleeping with her ex-husband and planned to go back with him. Which, by the time it happened, came mostly as a relief.

***

Fifteen months would pass this way: weeks-long bouts of loneliness interspersed by work, blackjack, every-other-weekend fatherhood, and fleeting, fiddling romantic ventures. Then one Saturday morning in early December, staring out at the sort of gray, snow-flecked fog that only happens during winters at the shore, and three days into another vigil of dark windows and darker thoughts, Harry's will suddenly failed him. And he called Touch of Class.

The voice that answered this time was a man's, slurred and nasally, with an edge of impatience. Harry asked to make an appointment with Dawn.

"Who's this?" The voice asked.

Harry said it was Bobby Robbins, the name they'd agreed on.

"*The fuck it is,*" the voice said. "I know who you are, asshole. She don't want to talk to you. And don't call here no more, hear? Don't call no more or you'll wish you hadn't." And he hung up.

Three days later a letter arrived, addressed in the precise, cursive script of a schoolgirl:

> *Dear Harry:*
> *I am sorry I never answered your calls. I have thought about it, and really think it would be best for us not to see each other, and that you not try to call me again. Please do not worry about me, as I am doing fine. I hope you can understand, and that you are happy and well.*
>
> > *Dawn*

Twelve

_____

July 2017

B y the end of the third week, they had developed a routine. Sarah would see the psychologist on Mondays, the rehab counselor Wednesdays, and the internist every two weeks to monitor progress— plus the twenty-minute daily walk she'd promised. She was taking the bus three times weekly to a volunteer gig Harry had gotten her, sorting food and clothes at a homeless shelter (the Costco job would come later), and meeting him for dinner twice a week.

Most times when he saw her, it seemed to Harry that she was making progress. She had gained weight and was less tired than she'd been and less moody; the anti-depressant she was on was plainly having an effect. Lately, though, she had seemed oddly jumpy, even fearful. The week before, she'd insisted on buying a second deadbolt lock for her motel room door; the last time they'd gone out to dinner, she'd wanted to take a seat in view of the entrance—and when none was available, she'd spent much of the meal glancing twitchily over her shoulder. When Harry asked why, she'd answered strangely: "You never know who's out there," then dismissed the subject with a nervous laugh.

For Harry it was a confusing time. She seemed in so many ways piti-able—and yet there remained this shadow, never far off, of the Sarah he remembered. There would be some moment: It might be in her smile, or the way she looked at him, or even just the way she rose from a table or moved her hands when she talked. He was always recognizing things. And he would feel this small quiver, this surge of feeling—and then it would fade and the real Sarah, the decrepit, diminished Sarah, would take over. It was a strange, off-balance feeling, like being in two places at once.

She claimed to have stopped drinking, and had promised to cut the pills in half. She said she'd had a call with her daughter, and that they'd talked about getting a place together (though Harry suspected this might be more wishful than real). Beyond this, she gave no sign of knowing, or caring, what the future might hold—though it did seem that she might be on a path to having one. She was trying, anyway.

Toward the end of July, a piece at a time, she began sharing with Harry disconnected scraps of her past. At first only small stories: moments or encounters she remembered, a short-term alliance, the kindness of a stranger. Until one evening at a surf n' turf place they often chose, when Harry asked again how she'd managed in the years since Atlantic City. And this time there came an answer.

"What do you *think?* The only way I knew how."

Harry said nothing. Almost a minute passed before she spoke again. When she did it was a while before she stopped.

For the first "ten or twelve years," she said, she'd worked as an escort in New York, Memphis, Miami Beach, Atlanta, and Los Angeles. Twice she'd done jail time, once as long as three months: "But it wasn't too bad. And I got to read a lot."

In Miami, she'd met a john who said he wanted to help her.

"We used to meet every week. He told me he was in love with me, he said I was his 'inspiration,' that he'd marry me if he wasn't already married. He was a sweet man. But so sad too, so lonely. He'd cry some-times when we were together. I felt sorry for him."

After a time, she said, the man got her a job at the printing com-pany he owned—$250 a week to do billing and filing, plus what he paid her on the side:

"It was great for a while. Then one day he told me he didn't want me sleeping with anybody else. I told him I couldn't do that, and he went kind of nuts, he said he was going to kill himself. That was on a Friday. The next Monday I came into work and there was my check and a note that said I wasn't needed anymore."

From what Harry could tell, that took things into the early 2000s (she mentioned that she was working at the printing company when 9/11 happened). After she lost her job, Sarah said, she "got really depressed," began drinking heavily and snorting meth:

"It got so I'd have a drink first thing every morning—vodka, mixed with Sprite usually—then snort some ice, and I'd drink and stay high all day, or until the bottle was gone. Then I'd go to bed, and the next morning I'd buy another bottle and some more stuff and start again."

At one point, she said, when she was too broke to buy what she needed and was having trouble making rent, she passed up her escort job (which required splitting her fees with the agency) and took directly to the streets:

"I only did it for about two weeks. It was pretty scary; you could get knocked around if you didn't watch yourself. But it was easy money—twenty-five bucks for a blowjob in the car, three minutes and you're done. And I got to keep what I made."

Harry knew the scene she was describing: skanky, wasted women in low-cut polyester dresses, stumbling drunk or half-gone on junk, hustling drivers at red lights along Pacific Avenue in Atlantic City or on 10th Avenue in Manhattan, then disappearing with their johns down one-way alleys to do their business. They were the lowest rank of hookers, the "no-hopers," as he had written of them once: desperate, dirty, often diseased and usually too wasted to care. The image of Sarah as one of them felt unthinkable.

He tried not to react. But she had read his face.

"Don't look so holy, for God's sake. You of all people ought to know what I am."

"So tell me, what are you?"

"*I'm a used-up old whore.* No use to anybody, no use to myself." Her tone was almost matter-of-fact.

"So what would you *like* to be?" Harry asked then. "If you could do anything, go anywhere, what would you want it to be?"

She mused on this for a second, then answered almost cheerily.

"I'd be sixteen again—start all over again."

She tried to smile, but it came off as more of a wince.

"No, not sixteen, that was a shitty year . . . Maybe twenty-six? . . . Yeah, twenty-six wasn't too bad. Wasn't that about when *you* came along?"

The smile was real now—it was one of those moments—and Harry's mind flipped back to the times of earlier Sarah teases ("*I really am a siren, you know*"). But she had opened a door, intentionally or not, which felt like an invitation.

"What was wrong with sixteen? Why such a shitty year?"

"Oh God, Harry"—and here she let out a long mock-sigh. "Still the reporter, aren't you? Still can't leave anything alone."

"I stopped being a reporter a long time ago. I'd just really like to know."

Another sigh. "Okay . . . Sixteen was the year my father died. Of cancer. He was in prison."

"For what?"

"For molesting me. For raping me. Actually, I don't even remember what the exact charge was, what they called it in the end. But he went to prison."

Her voice was flat, her face a blank. Harry stumbled to find words.

"Oh God, Sarah. . . . For how long?"

"Ten years. But he never served most of it. He died after only about four."

"How old were you when he raped you?"

She lowered her head, then shook it dismissively.

"It wasn't actually rape—that's just what they called it. And not just once. More like a hundred times. But he didn't call it that. He called it *making love*. He wanted me to call it that too, and I didn't know any different, at least in the beginning. He said we were in love—I wanted to believe that, I didn't want to feel ashamed. And sometimes it almost felt that way. He was good to me, he bought me things, he took me on trips, he played games with me, he made me laugh. He called me his precious flower."

Harry could feel the revulsion rising like a knot in his throat. For a long time neither of them spoke.

"It started when I was ten or eleven, I think. Or maybe before that."

"How did it end? Did you tell somebody?"

"His girlfriend walked in on us. She went to the police. They made me testify."

"You didn't want to?"

"No, I hated it. I told you, he was good to me. I didn't want to be the reason he went to prison."

"You must have been pretty confused."

"I don't know. All I remember feeling was sad."

All this still as flat as though she were reading off a list. The same deadpan she'd used years before, when she'd described the atrocities she endured that night on the houseboat, and later when she spoke about her hooker dates, how they worked and what they paid. Like it was part of someone else's history. It seemed not to reach her at all.

"What happened then? Your mother was gone already, right? You were still just a kid." Harry had learned this at an earlier dinner, that her mother had left when she was a child.

"The girlfriend took me in for a while, but that was a bust. So I went to live with my uncle."

She paused here, and shook her head again, as though she were done talking. Then she continued, but in a voice now not much louder than a whisper.

"He helped me go to college, this little Podunk place in upstate New York, which lasted half a year. But it turned out he was a jerk . . .

"Listen, Harry, can we just cut this? I know you care, but I don't want to answer any more questions. There's no more to tell anyway."

It was late by then, the tables around them had emptied, the waitress had delivered the check. Sarah seemed suddenly very tired. Harry didn't know if the talking—or the remembering—had worn her out, or if she was drawing a line on things. Her flatness made it impossible to tell the difference. Which may have been how it felt for her as well.

He ached for her. For the awful unfairness of her sixty-one years. He went to sleep that night wondering if she'd ever in her life been held, uncomplicatedly held, by anyone who wanted nothing from her—not her body or her beauty or the money she made for them. If she'd ever been held just for love. Or if she even knew the difference.

Then it occurred to him that he might have come the closest.

***

He had volunteered long before, as he had several times in the past, to teach in that year's summer program. Though it was a limited curriculum—Harry taught only two classes—the campus was soon his surest solace. He taught harder, lingered over lesson plans and at department meetings, found excuses to remain in his office sometimes well into the evening. When a student stopped by to talk about an upcoming paper or the injustice of last week's C, he was seldom too busy to oblige—and often found himself segueing into some story about how it was to be a journalist ("We called ourselves reporters then") back in the days of glue pots and copy spikes.

For the few with the interest or simple kindness to listen, he could go on for half an hour about the loud, smoky newsrooms he had been a part of, and the boozy men at their Royal Manuals ("My earliest mentors, nearly all of them gone now.") who told crude sexist jokes and badgered their sources from rotary phones with cords like copulating snakes but could give you four fifteen-inch stories on anything you needed before they broke for lunch.

He was seen by most of his students, he knew, as a full-fledged dinosaur. But he didn't mind. It was a fair assessment: His journalism career was decades behind him by then—CNN had been a youngster, the Web was barely a blip. The kindest thing you could call him was a purist.

Every once in a while, when the moment and the student mix both felt right, he would wander off into ancient history: about Vietnam or Watergate, Selma or the '68 assassinations. Or even Joe Cocker, Dylan or The Stones, and how their music had fueled a generation. He could go on all class about that. And it was always a hit with the students.

Sometimes he would wind up with a piece of personal history: about how the combined weight of all that injustice and moral outrage had opened his eyes to himself. And how, by the end of the summer of 1973, between his junior and senior years of college—which he'd spent sweeping up shavings in a Colorado sawmill—he had known for sure how he wanted to make his living.

He said nothing about the years just prior to his coming to teach at the college—the "lost years," as he referred to them with Julia and one or two close friends. There had been almost ten of them, after Atlantic City, during which he had stumbled through life mostly without planning or even thinking, sometimes more drunk than sober, living in short-term rentals, working at short-term jobs—the longest was a two-year gig outside Boston driving an airport shuttle. Toward the end of this time, he'd begun a half-hearted re-entry into journalism with some freelance magazine pieces, most of them for an alternative weekly in Cambridge. It was one of these, about a homeless teenage couple "hustling crack and living between seasonal hibernations" that had touched Julia's heart and brought them together. But other than that, those years, in Harry's view, were best forgotten.

As for Atlantic City itself, he said almost nothing. Only that he had worked a while for the daily there, that some things he wrote hurt people he never meant to hurt, and that he had left because of it.

Thirteen

——

For Harry in those years, the cruelest month was always March. The wind came in chilling blusters, the dark days seemed endless, the salt air off the beach felt like an out-of-season insult. On the streets of Atlantic City, the muddy slush from casino buses slapped and slithered at your feet. Along a near-empty Boardwalk, ragged strings of swaddled people scurried between casino entrances. Outside the Resorts casino, in that final, awful March of 1987, a billboard the length of an eighteen-wheeler, its torn edges flapping in the wind, exhorted you to "Remember: Your Life Begins Now."

Harry would remember that billboard always. And that March.

The years, and the stories, were running together: an endless ribbon of rigged contracts, crooked mayors, evicted families, the never-ending suicides of broken gamblers. It felt sometimes to Harry—with Sarah's crazy, beautiful energy no longer in his life—like the air itself was filthy and had infected him, as though he was being slowly eaten alive.

But he loved the column. As much as he could hate the filth it so often depicted—and even sometimes hate writing about it—more than anything else in those months it filled his life. It defined him.

Then, one Monday morning that March, less than a year after its birth, the column was no more.

Six months earlier, Harry had written one about the effect of casinos on the lives of local working-class gamblers: how, with the dice or slots now only a short car trip away, weekly paychecks, for some, were disappearing. Five weeks after it ran, the family of one of his sources, a postman from Millville, sued the paper, alleging that Harry had depicted him as an addicted gambler, causing him "irreparable reputational damage." Not long after the story ran, the man's fifteen-year-old daughter, ostracized at school, had "slashed her wrists in an attempt to take her life."

The daughter eventually recovered, and the paper settled out of court. Harry never learned the details of the settlement, and Alcorn was sympathetic ("You did your job—it coulda happened to anybody"). Within days, though, came a memo from the publisher: the column was to be scrapped; Harry would return to his previous beat writing features, which would be subject to "scrupulous hands-on editing."

Outside of this, nothing was said. It was a dispassionate defrocking, but he felt it every time he walked through the newsroom.

***

With little now to fill his evenings, Harry found himself at the black-jack tables—usually at Caesars, now his favorite—more often than before. It was almost always a weekday, between five and six in the afternoon. This was the lull-hour: the day-trippers filing out for their buses, the evening crowd not yet arrived. At table after table, idle, dull-eyed dealers stood cross-armed behind banks of chips whose value could put a child through college. An hour later, the seats would be three-quarters full, and in the craps pit the howlers would be howling. But at five-thirty on a Tuesday or Wednesday of a winter afternoon, you could choose between tables and have your choice of seats.

On an early evening in late March, two weeks after his wing-clipping at *The Herald*, Harry was in an end seat at a ten-dollar table, playing alongside an intense, college-age guy in a baseball cap and a woman in her fifties with a weathered face and two inches of aging cleavage. He was losing: down half his stake by the end of an hour, and thinking already about going home. The young man, who was betting the minimum $10 on every hand and flexed and unflexed his fists with each new card, appeared to be losing as well. The woman, her mouth twisted around a cigarette the length of a pencil and with what looked like a glass of scotch at her elbow, was hunched over her cards like a widow over her knitting, hand and arm the only proof of life: smoke, drink, bet, stand or hit. She was betting between $50 and $100 a hand, but clearly knew nothing of strategy, or didn't care—she hit twelves against the dealer's five, and randomly split face cards. Yet she won continually.

At one point, the dealer, a sultry Black girl with the bored disdain of a punk-rock waitress, dealt herself a blackjack. Her arm fanned the table, sweeping up chips like wind across grass. The indifference hurt to watch.

"Not so fast, hon," said the cleavage woman, "I got one, *too*."

The dealer glanced at the woman's cards, an ace and a ten, then replaced her chips as briskly as if she'd planned the error. "Sorry," she said, tonelessly, sweeping the cards from the table without looking up. "Didn't see your hand, is all."

"That's okay, hon," the woman said. "As long as one of us did."

Harry glanced at her stack. There was more than $2,000 there, in green and black chips. He was down to less than $200 by then, most of it in reds. Normally he managed to not be distracted by the players around him, but this woman's ridiculous luck, coupled with her awful play, was beginning to gnaw at his nerves. And it must have shown.

"You're sweating, babe," the woman said to him suddenly, as the dealer shuffled between shoes. "Maybe you oughtta take a break."

The young man, sitting at the opposite end, peered from one of them to the other, squinting narrowly as though reading small print from a distance, then looked away.

"Just play your own cards, lady," Harry answered back, as coldly as he could manage. "I sweat, you split face cards. We all have our quirks."

She ignored this. "How much you down?"

Her tone was suddenly almost gentle, and Harry saw now that her face, though too heavy with makeup, was striking in a seasoned sort of way. She looked like a slightly older version of Anne Bancroft in *The Graduate*.

"Enough," Harry said. He didn't know why he'd answered at all.

"Well, don't sweat it, okay? I was down more than a grand two hours ago. The cards can turn on a dime. . . . But you know that, right?"

When there was no answer, she persisted:

"So how do I *know* that you know that? Huh? Aren't you gonna ask me that?"—it was clear to Harry now that she was drunk, or on her way to being.

"Because you're *Harry Hopper*, right? Harry Hopper the columnist, the reporter, the whatever-you-call-yourself, who knows all about *everything*, 'cause he's been around the block *so-o-o-o many times*. You look just like your picture, Harry. Maybe not quite as good-looking."

This wasn't an uncommon experience for him around town. Normally he'd ignore it, but this woman plainly wasn't going to be put off—although she seemed less hostile than amused.

"You must be local," he said. "Nobody north of Tom's River would know me from Adam."

"Yeah, I'm local," the woman answered. "Not originally, and not real happy about it sometimes. But yeah, I'm as local as you get."

The dealer had finished her shuffle, and was tapping the little circle in front of Harry, awaiting his bet. He put down four reds—$20—and was dealt an eighteen. The dealer showed two queens, a twenty. Her arm, as though switch-activated, did that wind-across-grass sweep again—and all at once the will just left him. He stood up, gathered his coat from the back of the chair and began to stuff his modest stack of chips into his pants pocket.

"Calling it a night," he mumbled to the woman. All he wanted at that moment was to be gone.

He wasn't sure she'd even heard him, and didn't care, but she answered right away: "Good idea. Maybe I will, too. How about I buy you a drink?"

Harry's coat was on by now. He barely looked at her.

"No thanks. I'm heading home."

"Home? . . . You mean to your little place on North Raleigh? The one with the closet-sized bathroom?"

He was sure he'd never seen the woman before, but tried to stay unruffled.

"Do I know you from somewhere? Or are you stalking me, or what?"

"Neither one, babe."

She was smiling widely now, and seemed to be enjoying herself, though as she tried to stand up he could see that she was drunker than he'd thought.

"Never seen you before in my life, and wouldn't waste my time stalking you. We have a common friend, is all."

"And who would that be?"

"Nancy Donnelly. I'm sure you remember Nancy?"

Harry flashed back to the last image he had of the trim, pretty woman he'd dated briefly the winter before, the once and future wife of a casino exec, sitting on the edge of his bed trying not to cry.

"Don't look so shocked," the woman said. "Nancy didn't share any dirty little secrets if that's what you're thinking. At least none you need to worry about . . . So, you gonna let me buy you that drink?"

***

They walked together through the casino, which was filling by then and growing louder, up the escalator to the Rolling Chair Lounge, named for the wicker-backed chairs on wheels that surrounded its tables and that once, in grander days, were pushed for a nickel a ride by twelve-year-old Black boys who were tipped an extra nickel to whistle as they pushed. But the woman walked straight to the bar.

"Courvoisier stinger on the rocks," she told the bartender. Harry asked for a bourbon straight up.

"I'm Claire Cellini." She took his hand in hers and pumped it once. "Pleased to meet you, Harry."

Harry looked at her. Her face was creased and deeply tanned, with the kind of half-ruined beauty you saw sometimes in the former Miss Americas who came to Atlantic City every year at pageant time to pose alongside the current queens, hoping to match freshness with classicism.

"You wouldn't know my name, but I think you would my husband's . . . Sy Cellini? I believe he's known to you as '*The bloodsucker*'? He got a real kick out of that column. It's still hanging in his office."

"*You're Sy Cellini's wife?*"

Harry saw in his mind the bulbous face of the developer who had sold a half-acre Pacific Avenue parking lot to a Nevada casino syndicate for $3.5 million. Within four months of the sale, the steel skeleton of what was to be the city's newest casino stood on the site of Cellini's old lot. That was three years before: the girders were still in place, a rusting, three-story eyesore at the north end of the avenue—the syndicate had run out of financing along the way, then skulked out of town without so much as a press release.

But Cellini's millions had grown with the city. He owned a restaurant there now, and another on the mainland, a condo complex in Somers Point, and twenty-odd properties in the North Inlet, where his name was an obscenity to the Blacks and Hispanics who paid their rents to him—or worse, had lost homes or possessions (or in one case an infant daughter) to the fires of "undetermined origin" that periodically ravaged his properties. Cellini, whom Harry had never met but knew by reputation, was the vilest of slum landlords in a city known for them.

"That's right, babe. I'm the bloodsucker's wife. But don't worry, no offense taken. Sy loves publicity of any kind. To be honest, he doesn't have much of a conscience about things. Insults only amuse him."

"He couldn't afford to have a conscience," Harry said coldly. "He wouldn't last a week in this town."

"You got *balls*, Harry. Just like Sy. Only he owns half the city and you sweat bullets over a twenty-dollar bet."

"We don't all march to the same drummer, I guess."

"So who's your drummer, Harry? The Good Samaritan?"

The woman seemed to have sobered up some, her speech now quicker and less garbled.

"No one your husband would know."

"Don't count on it. You have a thing or two in common. You both chase tail, for one thing."

Up to that point, Harry had figured to ride all this out as a kind of adventure, one of those little side trips some of us take from time to time mostly just to see where they'll take us. But now he was angry.

"That's *bullshit*, and you know it. Nancy and I dated for a few weeks last winter. I wasn't married, and as far as I knew neither was she at the time. What's the point of all this anyway? Why'd you ask me here, just to dish up dirt?"

"No. I asked you here because you seemed like such a lost little boy down there. And because I was curious."

"Curious about what?"

"What you were like, whether you're as self-righteous in person as you are in print."

"And?"

"You try, but you can't cut it."

"Nancy tell you that?"

"Nancy liked you. She liked you a lot, if that makes any difference to you. But she also thought you were a confused, guilty romantic who didn't know which end was up."

Harry tried not to smile. That sounded like something that would have come from Nancy. "I suppose there's some truth to that," he said.

This seemed to calm the waters between them. For the next half-hour or so they talked about Nancy (who'd just moved to Las Vegas following her husband's promotion); about the casino industry, then about *The Herald*, which the woman said was far too sleepy in its coverage of the region.

Harry agreed. He liked her. Her directness appealed to him; her interest seemed genuine, almost beseeching, as though she were a friend, or wanted to be. He began to feel as he often did around such people: the need to be less wary, to offer more of himself without suspicion. His wife had always called it "going with the flow," and had said that if he could learn it he would come to see that the world was full of good people and offered more to explore than dark corners.

"So what's the paper got you working on these days?"

He told her briefly about the fiasco with the postman, and the downsizing he'd suffered. Then that he was working on a piece about a local boxer.

"That's too bad. I've always looked forward to your column—as much I think you're way too pious sometimes. To be honest, it might be the *only* thing in *The Herald* I look forward to reading . . . But tell me about your boxer. Isn't that a little off the track for you? Wouldn't that be more of a sports thing?"

"It would. Except it's not about boxing. It's more about this city, through his eyes. He grew up here, never been anywhere else. His career took off when casinos came in, then he pissed off some people, they busted him, and now he's delivering flowers."

"*Ohhhh*, yes, that sounds more like the Harry Hopper I know. Let me guess—he's Black, right? And poor, a victim of injustice? Hard times at the hands of the white establishment? Tell me I'm wrong."

"You're not wrong"—Harry was almost laughing at this point. "But don't be so cynical. Somebody needs to be writing this stuff."

"No question. And you're the perfect champion. Dedicated, selfless, committed to the downtrodden. You're a fool, Harry, but I like you. I see what Nancy saw in you . . . Have another drink, your glass is empty."

It was nearly eight o'clock. They were still alone at the bar, though the wicker chairs behind them were filling slowly, with couples mostly, for the lighting was soft and the chairs folded into themselves like rounded love seats. It was a pleasant place to be, gracious and vaguely faux historical.

Harry was glad he'd come. The woman was no threat now: an adventurer of a sort, not unlike him, and maybe just as lonely. He ordered for them both, and put a twenty on the bar—but she pushed it back and replaced it with her own.

"Tell me about your boxer. Does he have a name?"

"Tyrone Everett."

"Was he good?"

"For a local. He was ranked once."

"What happened?"

"He was supposed to throw a fight, and he wouldn't, so they pushed him out. At least that's what I've put together. I haven't been able to nail it down, though."

"How old is he?"

"Thirty-two or -three."

"Too old to fight again, I guess?"

"Maybe not. He's in pretty good shape, goes to the gym every day. It's the only real home he has."

"That big old place in the Inlet? The one that used to be a church?"

"That's the one. He's been going since he was a kid. It's run by an old guy who's like a father to him."

"I know that gym. It's on the same block as a couple of Sy's lots. He tried to buy it once, but the owner wouldn't sell."

"You mean Resorts. I'm not surprised. They'd never let it go, they use it as a training gym for the fighters they book."

"Not if we're talking about the same gym."

"The Lucky Lady? On New Jersey off Baltic?"

"That's it. It's owned by a man named McGuigan, and he's local. Resorts may be the owner on paper, but that kind of stuff happens all the time in this town—as I'm sure you of all people would know."

"Vic McGuigan? The promoter?"

"That's right. I met him, in fact. Sy had him over to the house, to try to talk him into selling the place. But his price was way out of line. Not only that, he wanted Sy to buy out the contract on the guy he's got running it. The old guy you're talking about."

"Toby? Toby Ward works for McGuigan?"

Harry's mind flashed on the image of Tyrone, then on his child's faith in the man he called his father; and his world of The Lucky Lady with its "lotta love," and Eel and DeWayne and all the rest.

"Guess that's news to you, huh?"

"Not the way I heard it, is all."

He felt weak. His night was done. He thanked the woman for the drink, swallowed the last of it, and got up to leave. The woman motioned to the bartender for another.

"Nancy was right about you, Harry," she said as he pulled on his coat. "You're a sweet man, but you're in way over your head."

When he reached the exit and looked back, the woman was talking to the bartender and gesturing toward the seat he'd just left. They were both laughing. When she saw him looking, she waved gaily.

Fourteen

———

It was a lousy night out, cold and sleeting with an east wind blowing in hard off the ocean. Leaving the Caesars parking garage, the sleet was coming down diagonally, forming inch-deep mush piles on the sidewalks. On Pacific Avenue, the traffic lights shimmered off empty streets like colored balls.

Ten minutes west in Egg Harbor Township, just past the traffic circle that marks the outer limit of the city's modest sprawl, the parking lot of Club Thirty was close to full. The Thirty was a press bar. There was one like it, in those days, in every town large enough to support a daily: dark and cool and vaguely grimy, with a long burnished oak bar that served a dozen or so stools, and some tables in the back that, no matter how heavy the crowd, almost no one ever used. Because the bar was the place to be, its walls lined with yellowed clippings of big events in the city's history—the jailing of old bosses, the coming of the airport, the advent of casinos. Curled photos of long-gone reporters, each with a chummy message or short published tribute to the place, were tacked on a board behind the bar.

The faces at this time of night—two hours after quitting time for

The Herald's day crew—were always about the same: chain-smoking young reporters haranguing meaningfully over beers; young entertainment writers, brittle and churlish but privately star-struck; and the older ones, the editors and wire-editors, sports writers and twenty-year veterans—nearly all men—who drank more, talked less and always got the empty stools.

It had been weeks since Harry's last visit there—his demotion at *The Herald* wasn't something he felt like answering questions about—and he had at first resisted the urge to go. But walking through the door that night felt, to his surprise, a little like coming home.

Almost the first face he saw was the one he'd come to see: Jack Duffy, still holding down *The Herald's* casino beat, and still pursuing his war of words with Donald Trump. He was one of those people who work hard at being aloof, and he could be fiercely caustic at times—especially when he was drinking—but he knew the city, its skeletons and secrets and private alliances, probably better than anyone in the newsroom. If anyone could confirm or refute Claire Cellini's version of things, it would be Duffy.

He was on his feet behind the seated tier of elders at the bar, his forearm on the shoulder of a young reporter, talking in what looked like guarded tones—a standard effect for Duffy—into the woman's ear. Judging by his slouch and the droop of his eyelids, Harry guessed he was on his third or fourth scotch.

They had been loose friends for years and had shared, over time, most of the confidences divorced male reporters share: work, women (though Duffy knew nothing of Sarah), book dreams, the fear of growing stale. Harry liked him, though their friendship existed almost solely around drink.

"*Well, lookee here!*"—it was among Duffy's stock greetings. "The illustrious 'Boardwalk Breslin.' How you been, old sport?"

He was farther gone than Harry had thought, but introduced him to the young reporter, who smiled warmly, said something kind about his column, then quickly drifted away.

Harry ordered a bourbon. The two talked briefly of newsy things: Nicky Scarfo's upcoming trial for murder and extortion—he would spend the rest of his life in federal prison—Donald Trump's latest skirmish with Harrah's casino, the last mayor's jail sentence, the new one's passel of cronies. Harry proposed they shoot some pool again some time, as they had several times the year before at a redneck bar further inland. Duffy said he'd like that, and they agreed to make a plan.

It wasn't long before Harry found his opening: He'd heard rumors of Resorts selling the Inlet gym to Vic McGuigan. Was there anything to that? Had McGuigan ever owned it at all?

Duffy was quiet for a moment, then shook his head in mock perplexity.

"You that hard up for a story these days? A shitty old gym in the Inlet?—not exactly what you'd call stop-the-presses stuff, is it?"

Harry said there was a boxer he might write a story about. He asked again what he knew about McGuigan.

Duffy drained his glass, reached over an old timer's shoulder and tapped the bar for another round.

"All the years you've been around, sport"—'sport' was Duffy's diminutive for any male under sixty—"there's sure a lot you don't know."

"Sounds like it. So you're saying he owns that gym?"

"I don't know if he owns it or not. But it wouldn't surprise me. Vic McGuigan owns a lot of things—depending on what you mean by 'own.' It's usually not his dough that bought it. And a lot of it's off the books."

Harry hadn't known that, and told him so.

"You've been doing your bleeding-heart gig too long, sport . . . McGuigan's thing with boxers is his front job. He's a fixer. He's got a piece of a lot of things—boxing, hookers, drugs, the numbers, just about any slimy shit you could name. Only he doesn't own most of it.

He's a frontman for Scarfo—or was, till Little Nicky got nailed. But he still fronts for the Philly mob. Buys and sells, works payoffs. But it's all handshake stuff, not the kinda things that get written down. You gotta have sources. Which obviously you *don't*."

He was right. It had been a long time since Harry, whose output lately had been almost all columns and features, had done the kind of grunt work Duffy was talking about—the kind that takes you past the press releases and public records into the netherworld of Duffy's "handshake stuff." And where the mob was concerned, that was the only world that counted for much.

"Could you maybe dig around a little for me?" Harry asked now. "See what you can find out about the gym?"

"Maybe. Where you planning to go with this story?"

"Like I told you, it's about this boxer. And the old guy, Toby, who runs the gym. I just need to know who owns the place, who's running the show there."

"So you're the Lone Ranger now, huh? Okay, fine. Just watch your ass, sport. You go sniffing around Vic McGuigan, you better know what you're doing."

***

Two days later, around four o'clock that Friday afternoon, Duffy pulled up a chair at Harry's desk at *The Herald*.

"I think I got what you're looking for, sport. How about we get out of here, head to The Thirty, talk about it over beers?" He seemed in a jovial mood.

Harry said he couldn't, that he had to leave soon to drive north, it was his weekend with Woody. (This wasn't true, but another night at The Thirty with a drunken Duffy seemed more than he could manage right then.) Duffy shrugged, then, with a show of diligent ceremony, pulled a notebook out of the beat-up brown satchel he carried everywhere with him, and flipped through some pages.

"So it's pretty much like you said. The gym's in McGuigan's name. But not only his. There's two other guys, too. One of 'em is that old guy you mentioned, Ward, Toby Ward, the trainer. And there's a third one, Ruben Florio, maybe you know who that is? Anyway, the three of them, they got, like, a third each. And it's actually down on paper, which you hardly ever see with these kinda guys."

He thumbed past another couple of pages. "But it's more than just the gym—it's a bunch of those boxers, too. Their contracts. There are four of 'em, maybe one of them is your guy . . . "

And he read the names from his notebook: Esteban Castillo, Tyrone Everett, Archie Johnson, and a fourth Harry didn't recognize.

"Those same three guys, they own a piece of their contracts, same three-way deal. But separate from the gym. They bought that from Resorts."

Harry's stomach had tightened into a ball. It all fit. Castillo was the fighter Tyrone was supposed to have lost to, Archie ("Peaches") Johnson the ranked middleweight Florio had promised would be his next fight.

Duffy handed him a Xerox of the paperwork he had, and said that Harry owed him one.

Harry asked if the contracts were dated.

"February twelfth, 'eighty-two, for all of it. Two hundred sixty grand for the gym. There's no record of a price for the fighters. But it looks like it was a package deal."

So the three of them had put together their own little syndicate, a week before Tyrone's last fight. It seemed pretty clear what the plan had been: In a bout arranged and promoted by McGuigan, Tyrone, taking his cue from his trainer, Florio (and later affectingly mollified by Toby), would lose to Castillo, a journeyman boxer, who'd been a seven-to-one underdog in Vegas. His own ranking would drop accordingly, which would make him even longer odds, maybe as high as ten-or twelve to-one, when he next faced Peaches Johnson, a top-ten middleweight who would then, more than likely, also be induced to lose.

On this pair of fights alone—never mind what they put together next, or where the fourth guy fit into the plan—Harry figured the three of them stood to make around fifteen dollars for every dollar wagered. There was no telling how much that would have been, or who else had been brought into the deal. But it seemed certain that the Scarfo group would have had a big piece of the pie.

And the risk was small. In a sport ungoverned by any league or authority, with few restrictions on the terms of a boxer's or promoter's contract—and with each fighter almost solely dependent on his handlers for counsel—the path had been paved for a killing.

Except Tyrone had won. And many thousands of dollars had probably been lost. It was hard to figure how he'd come away with all his limbs intact.

Harry thought of what Sarah had said: *Tyrone's lost everything he ever dreamed of. That's the only story there is.* She was right, of course. That was the only story he should care about now. But it wasn't. He wished it was—he truly wished it was—but it wasn't.

"So where does your boxer fit into all this?" Duffy asked then. "He one of the guys they bought? Somebody take a dive or something? It's gotta be something like that."

Harry told him what he knew. For the few minutes it took him, Duffy sat unmoving, like a skinny Buddha, eyes narrowed, hands folded in his lap. Then he opened his eyes, shook his head slowly and let out a long breath.

"*Whoa* . . . Yeah, that could be big. Only where's your proof the fight was rigged? Seems like you got nothing without somebody talking."

Harry said he thought he could get Tyrone to tell him on the record what he'd told him over burgers at the pub.

"How do you figure he'll do that?"

"He loves that old guy, Toby, like a father. When he finds out he was part of the group that sold him out, he's gonna go nuts . . . I think he trusts me. I think he'll give me what I need."

Duffy took another long breath. "Wow. That's kind of rough, don't you think? Whatever happened to the old high-minded Harry?"

"I'm going after a story, Duff. Same as you would."

"Well, damn . . . Sounds like you've joined the club, sport—you want a story, sometimes you gotta be a fuckin' *sleaze*."

Harry wouldn't remember what he said next, or if he said anything at all. The keyboards went on clicking at every desk around them; the green shimmer of VDT screens color-washed the air, a reporter somewhere was talking on the phone. All he would remember was that word.

Fifteen

———

July 2017

Sarah applied for a part-time job at Costco, using a fake Texas driver's license she'd bought online for $100 ("so maybe the hooker arrests won't show up," she would tell Harry). They called the next day to ask when she could start.

It was a warehouse job, unpacking and coding produce, sometimes stocking shelves. The pay was $11.50 an hour, eighteen hours a week. There was a local bus route that took her to and from work.

"I feel like I'm getting a whole new life," she said after the first day.

Through all of that week, Harry would tell the police later, she was "literally giddy" each time he saw her. During week two, she seemed "a little edgy, a little preoccupied"; she said that things at work were stressful, that she thought her boss might be expecting too much. When Harry had asked for an example, she shrugged and said to forget it.

Then, on the morning of July 20th, the second workday of her third week on the job, she arrived at work complaining of dizziness, worked fitfully for the next hour, then turned suddenly white and passed out on the warehouse floor. When a coworker went to help her, she sat up, mumbled a string of disconnected words and passed out again. The store manager called an ambulance. Harry got a call from St. Joseph's Hospital in Nashua and was there in twenty minutes.

"She was pretty out of it when she came in," the ER doctor told him. "Looks like she OD'd on a mix of hydrocodone and a benzo, Valium maybe. And she's been doing it for a while, her GI system is pretty messed up."

She was conscious by the time Harry got to her, but only barely. Secured in a gurney just off the ER with an IV drip in place, she was halfway delirious, wide-eyed and plainly frightened, mumbling things that made no sense at all.

"Who are you? Why are you here? Are you working for him?"

"Sarah, it's Harry. Harry. You're in the hospital. I came to see you. You passed out at work."

"Harry? . . . Yes, Harry. But you don't work for him, do you?"

"I don't work for anyone, Sarah. I'm here to see you. I'm here to take care of you."

This seemed to relax her, but only for a second. Then her eyes widened again and her face froze into a terrified grimace. Her next words were a garble: something about someone she said she'd seen at work, someone who had "found" her there.

"How did he find me, Harry?"

"How did *who* find you, Sarah?"

More garbled words. Then the word "uncle" followed by what sounded like "broke" or "poke." Harry reached down and stroked her hair. "Thank you," she mumbled. "You're good to me." And she fell asleep.

That was when the shadows began to overtake her. She would go back to work a week later, and enroll in the drug rehab program the hospital referred her to, and some days it would seem that she might be turning a corner—she could still laugh at her own silly jokes, and sink into reveries over the songs of Lucinda Williams or Loretta Lynn. But other things were different. It was as though a light had been switched off.

Just two days after the tox screens showed that the drugs were mostly out of her system, Harry began to suspect that she must be using again, maybe more heavily. She would sit in a restaurant for long seconds, staring out the window, not saying a word. Her responses to his questions were nothing like before, when she'd skipped around them with jokes or distractions—now she would just look at him sadly and shake her head, smile weakly and say it didn't matter. She seemed indifferent to everything, indifferent to the world.

Harry kept trying. He took her to dinner three times in a week, once with Julia, the other times alone. They went to the movies together, another time bowling—where Sarah squealed with delight, so familiarly it sent shivers up his spine, when all the pins went down. But always the darkness returned. Once in early August, he invited her to stay over in his little guest room—only to find her, at five in the morning, fully clothed, staring out the living room window in the darkness toward the river.

There was one more episode at work. It came on a Wednesday, not long after she'd returned to the job. It was four p.m., quitting time for Sarah's shift—as her supervisor, Patty, would describe it to Harry:

"The normal thing was, she'd leave out the warehouse door with the others, walk the couple blocks to catch her bus. That day, though, she walks to the door, takes one step out toward the parking lot, turns every shade of white like she's just seen a ghost, then turns 'round and runs back inside, whimpering like a brand-new puppy or something . . .

"So I ask her, 'What's wrong, honey? What's wrong?'—'cause she's a nice lady, she sometimes talks to me. And she points at this car outside in the lot, this old blue Caddy that's parked there with some old guy at the wheel, probably waiting for a customer or something. 'There he is again,' she says. 'There he is, I knew he'd come back.'"

"So I say to her, 'Who is he, honey?' But she won't say nothing, just shakes her head. So I end up taking her out the back way, through the store, and walking her to her bus. And she's shaking the whole way, holding onto my arm like a baby."

***

At a little after midnight on a Friday a week later, Harry, alone at home, was awakened by a high-pitched keening from behind his house, which he took at first to be the yowling of a rutting cat.

He found Sarah in the backyard, halfway between his deck and the river, squatting on the ground in shorts and a sweaty green T-shirt, one sneaker gone, her hair in wet strings. He let her in the backdoor. Her weeping by then had softened to guttural moans followed by sobs that shook her head and shoulders. He had no idea how she'd gotten there; there were no buses running at that hour.

He sat her down at his kitchen table and poured her a glass of milk; she drank it down without stopping to breathe. After a while the sobbing slowed.

"Tell me what happened, Sarah."

Her words came out almost robotically, in a voice he barely recognized.

"I killed him . . . I did it. I killed him . . . What else could I do?"

"You killed who?"

"I had to, I couldn't help it. I couldn't stand it anymore."

"Who are you talking about, Sarah?"

"You know. My daddy . . . But I had to . . . I had to."

"Your daddy died in prison, Sarah. You told me that yourself."

"No. I killed him. I stabbed him—so many times, so many times. I heard him die. It sounded like a frog."

She was panting now, in short, panicked breaths. Harry didn't know what to do. He poured her another glass of milk, and rubbed her back gently from behind while she drank it.

"We need to get you help, Sarah. I'm taking you to the hospital in the morning."

Her body contorted violently sideways in the chair, twisting to face him.

"NO! Please no hospital! I'll kill myself if you try!"

"Sarah, we've got to get you off the drugs. For good this time . . . Let me help you, *please*."

She didn't answer. Harry watched as she drew herself up in the chair. Her body was rigid. Suddenly he was terrified.

"Don't you want to know the story?"

"What story?"

"About why I killed him."

"I don't think you killed anyone, Sarah."

"You don't understand, I need you to understand. Please try to see . . . I had to do it. I had to, I had to."

She went on like this for several minutes, begging him to believe her, asking that he understand. But it seemed somehow to calm her. The longer she went on, the quieter and more resolute she seemed to become. And the more Harry began to wonder if—crazy or not, drug-addled or not, and however muddled her memories—something might really have happened.

"Why don't you tell me about it?"

For most of the next half-hour, now with her voice flat and faraway, she sat at Harry's kitchen table, telling her story while he stood across from her leaning against the refrigerator door. It was true what she had told him earlier, she said, that her father (always "Daddy" in her telling) had gone to prison for abusing her. She had lived during those years with an uncle—"Uncle Poke"—and his girlfriend in a town nearby. Every week she went with them to visit her father at the prison, which was not far from where they lived and where she'd grown up, in "this dump of a town" in upstate New York.

Harry thought he knew the name. "Your uncle Poke," he said. "Is that who you were talking about at the hospital that night? I couldn't tell, you were pretty out of it, but—"

"You're interrupting me," Sarah said sharply. "I'm trying to tell you something and you're interrupting me."

Her father, she said then, hadn't died of cancer in prison, as she'd claimed. Instead he'd been released after "maybe about two years" and returned home. The court wouldn't let him live with Sarah, so she had remained with the uncle in the nearby town and visited her father on weekends. She was in middle school by then.

"The visits were supposed to be supervised by my uncle, but sometimes they weren't, usually 'cause he was too busy drinking."

For the first several months, she said, the weekends with her father had gone well enough. "We went to places together, he bought me stuff, like before. He'd tell me over and over how sorry he was about things. He said it was wrong, that he wasn't really like that, and that he'd make it up to me. He was really sweet. Anyway, I guess in the end I believed him."

Then things took a turn, she said. It was the late 1960s; the region was deep in a recession. Sarah's father, who'd found work as a welder for a local Ford plant, was laid off.

"He started drinking a lot more—they all drank like fishes anyway—and we stopped going places. And some weekends I'd get there and he'd be so gone he couldn't get up off the couch, so I'd have to cook for him. Then he began getting really sloppy with his talk, asking me questions about my bra size and my period and saying how pretty I was and all. I was scared. But I didn't want to say anything 'cause I knew it'd make him mad—he could get pretty crazy when he was drinking. And I just kept telling myself how it was gonna be okay, how he was sorry for what he did and he didn't want to go back to prison . . .

"Then one night he just went at me. We were sitting at different ends of the couch watching TV—*Columbo*, he really liked *Columbo*—and he just puts his bottle down on the floor and comes across and grabs me and starts kissing me and feeling me and all. I screamed. I tried to push him off, I said if he didn't stop I'd tell Uncle Poke. I'd tell the social worker . . .

"He punched me in the face, so hard it almost knocked me out. He said he was gonna do what he wanted with me and I wasn't gonna tell anybody anything. And how he knew I liked it anyway. Then he just ripped off my pants and . . and he did it.

"When he was done he got up and grabbed my arm and twisted it behind my back hard, and told me if I didn't tell him I liked it he'd break it and the other arm too. He did that—he made me say I liked it, he made me say 'I like it, Daddy.' Then he went into the bedroom and passed out."

All this Sarah recounted without moving or looking up. When she stopped she raised her head and fixed Harry with a long, sad look, which she then—futilely, pathetically—tried to turn into a smile.

"Can I please have another glass of milk?"

"Sure." But Harry barely heard himself say it, and made no move from where he'd been standing, rigid now, feeling the pounding of his heart against his chest.

"What happened then?"

"Can I just have another glass of milk? I've always loved the taste of milk, ever since I was little. My mommy used to give it to me . . . I wish she hadn't gone away—everything would have turned out so different, you know? . . . But I hardly ever get to drink it anymore."

She was someone else now, somewhere else. Harry was unable for the moment to say or do anything but stare into the frightened, plaintive face that was looking up at him. Then he recovered himself, opened the refrigerator door and poured her a third glass of milk.

"So you killed him?"

She took a small sip, then placed her nose softly on the rim of the glass and closed her eyes. Her voice after that was so soft Harry had to lean close to understand.

"There was this big knife in the kitchen; I picked it up and took it in. I heard him snoring, on his back, snoring really loud. I hated him so much then, I wanted to stab him in the heart, and I was going to . . . But I couldn't do it. I just couldn't. I just stood there staring at him and crying like an idiot . . .

"Then he woke up, and he grabbed at me, he grabbed at my breasts and tried to pull me down . . . That was when I stabbed him. I stabbed him in the chest first, I think, or maybe the neck"—Sarah was sobbing softly now, repeating herself—"and he made this gurgling sound, like what a frog does. And I just kept stabbing him, over and over, I couldn't stop. There was blood everywhere."

She was silent again, her eyes open now, staring. Harry waited.

"I called Uncle Poke. I didn't know what else to do. He came over right away, with two men he knew, and took me back to his house. Then they went back and burned it down, they burned it all down."

"You mean?"—Harry was too stupefied to find his thoughts.

"The police came and talked to me afterward. I said I hadn't been there. I said I'd been at Uncle Poke's house when the fire happened. That's what he told me to say."

"What happened then?"

"Nothing. I stayed living with Uncle Poke."

Harry had other questions. Had there been no investigation? No autopsy? Was Uncle Poke a real uncle? Were things better living with him?

She didn't know about any investigations, she said, but no one would have told her anyway. Uncle Poke was her daddy's younger brother. His name wasn't really Poke; she didn't know his real one, but that was all anyone ever called him.

"For a while it was good. I wasn't scared anymore," she said. "Then it all changed back." Harry asked what she meant by this, but she just shook her head.

He tried asking again about the last incident at work. What had frightened her so much? Who did she think she'd seen in the parking lot? She squeezed her eyes shut tightly and shook her head again.

"I thought I saw Uncle Poke. But it wasn't really him."

Through it all, her head stayed lowered, her body almost inert. It was as though she were awaiting something. Judgement perhaps, or punishment.

Harry felt a surge of pity, followed seconds later by a memory he hadn't had in years: of Sarah that first night in 1984, in her slinky black dress, oozing sex and attitude at the mezzanine bar at Trump Plaza—*Oh, hi there, Mister Ace Reporter* . . .

For a moment it derailed him.

"*Who are you, Sarah? Who are you?* I want to help you. I want to understand you, but I don't know whether to believe you or not. Sometimes it feels like I don't even know who you *are*."

He half-expected her to turn on him, but instead she raised her head, looked at him and almost smiled.

"I don't know either . . . Maybe I'm two people. Sometimes I feel like that. Maybe I've always been two people."

"But how can I *help* you, Sarah?"

Her eyes dropped to her lap again and her voice faded to barely a whisper.

"Love me? . . . Maybe just love me?" It was the first time he'd ever heard her use that word.

"I *do* love you, Sarah. I always have."

"I'm glad," she said. "And can I please stay the night here?"

"Of course you can. And I'll fix you some breakfast in the morning."

"Okay. And then will you help me find my other sneaker?"

Sixteen

It was a little after seven o'clock when Harry left the paper that night. Duffy was long gone, headed for The Thirty. Any other night, Harry might have joined him, but now all he wanted was to be alone, he didn't much care where. He bought a fifth of good bourbon, a bottle of water, some paper cups and two fifty-cent bags of peanuts. Then he got on the Garden State and headed south. He had no idea to where.

Sleaze.

For the past two hours Duffy's word had been banging around in his head like a gavel thumping. He couldn't make it stop. Finally he pulled into a deserted rest area, broke open the bottle, poured half a cup's worth, and drank. Then breathed—drank and breathed, drank and breathed. He felt like crying but the tears wouldn't come.

It was a cold night, below freezing. There were no stars, no moon. When he turned off the headlights, the picnic table in front of him vanished into blackness. He left them off.

Everything felt broken. Dreams, beauty, innocence, loyalty, simple decency. All broken. He thought of the kid from Kenosha, years before, with his small, craps-game dream and his length of rubber hose, dead by the roadside a mile from where he was parked. Of a beautiful old man, a street minister he'd once interviewed, beaten almost to death over twelve dollars in his collection box. Of Tyrone and his blind, betrayed faith in the man he called his father. Of Sarah, grabbing at joy anywhere she could find it—dancing, bodysurfing, sex, a Ferris wheel—finally bullied into wanting only to die. So much wreckage. So much casual cruelty.

Maybe this was how it happened, he thought: You start out meaning no harm, wanting only to make your mark, earn your share, write your story. But in Atlantic City the scale of things is too big. There is too much of everything. Too much money too easily made or stolen, too much shimmer not to blind you, too many career-making stories to write and wrongs to try to set straight. And too much of all of it to keep a hold on however much conscience you have left.

Tyrone, Harry was almost sure, would tell him what he needed to hear. He would tell it in a fit of rage and pain, and Harry would write it down in his notebook and it would run in *The Herald* under a headline that would damn the people who ruled that world. And that would be fitting, that would be just. And what would happen then—to Tyrone, to Toby, to McGuigan, to the others—what would happen would happen. That would be the end of it. He would have told the story. He would have done his job.

He knew this wasn't even close to the whole truth. But he knew too that if he was to do what he was going to do, it was the only way it could be.

***

He fell asleep. When he awoke the bottle in his lap was half gone. The cold had deepened. There was no one on the Parkway but trucks.

He continued south, meaning to turn back at the next exit. But when he reached it, there seemed no reason not to keep driving. So he did: past the exits for Sea Isle City and its moped place, Seven-Mile-Beach at Stone Harbor (*U R FULL OF SHIT*), Avalon, Wildwood with its honky-tonk, then Wildwood Crest and Cape May Courthouse—till the Parkway ran out at land's end in Cape May.

From the exit at that hour, it was a five-minute drive to the beach. He drove slowly, making his way past the lines of B&B's and century-old Victorian mansions—all darkened now—till he came to the Admiral Benbow, the inn of two winters before, with its sad old man and his metal detector. He followed the driveway until it ended at the beach, and parked.

The inn was closed and boarded up—shut down for taxes, Harry would learn—its gravel parking lot pocked with icy puddles. The beach and the surf just beyond, in the car's headlights, were a gray froth of emptiness. Harry turned off the headlights, emptied what was left of the bourbon out the window, then sat for most of an hour, looking out through the blackness, listening to the surf, sipping water and chewing peanuts. Then he turned around and headed back north.

Seventeen

———

Tyrone's home was a block from the gym: a small, square room with one window, whose view was of a charred lot and two scrawny elms, on the second floor of what had once been a guesthouse for tourists of modest means. All but two rooms had been sealed off for years. Tyrone was now the sole tenant.

The only furniture was a faded pink dresser with decaled top, a plain wooden weight bench, a stuffed chair and a bed. The bed, which was a single, was covered in a heavy blue blanket. A framed picture of Tyrone's mother sat on the dresser. The only other decoration was a small poster tacked to the wall, announcing his first fight at Resorts, six years before, against someone named Titus Richards.

Harry hadn't seen Tyrone in nearly two months, and had never been to his place. He arrived there on a Sunday afternoon, two days after his meeting with Duffy, having gone first to the gym to learn that Tyrone hadn't been in all week.

"He probably at home if he ain't out taking care of his mama," Eel had told Harry. "He don't have no phone, but he don't generally mind when one of us come around."

The door was open when he reached the top of the stairs. Tyrone was on the floor inside, with his feet on the weight bench above him, doing sit-ups. He seemed unsurprised by Harry's arrival.

"Hey man, what's happening? Ain't seen you in a while."

Harry asked if he'd had lunch. Tyrone said he hadn't. So they walked the five minutes to the pub, and ordered the usual two burgers and a sub. Harry asked about Tyrone's mother.

"She about the same," he said. "Except they took off her leg, so she can't work no more. Outside of that, she about the same."

He said he had lived with her until two years before, when the house they'd shared on Oriental Avenue was gutted to make way for a low-income high-rise that still hadn't been built.

"I wished I was still there. Be easier to help her out that way. She don't get around too good, even before she lost the leg."

But he didn't mind where he was, he said. The rent was $120 a month, which he paid to the son of the old woman who lived alone on the first floor. He had seen her only once, but heard Johnny Carson through the floor every night, and her coughing, which "don't never seem to stop."

For the first half-hour, they ate their sandwiches and talked about the gym. Tyrone said he hadn't been going as much lately, but would again as soon as his mother didn't need him to take her for her treatments. He seemed different than before: quieter, less sure, less willful, almost a little lost. Harry told himself again—as he had already countless times—that no matter the pain in the meantime, in the end he would better off knowing the truth.

"I've done a little digging since the last time we talked," he said. "You were right about everything you told me. You got a really bad deal. By all rights you should still be fighting. And maybe you will be again."

And without waiting for the other man to interrupt or even react, he laid out the story, as flatly as he could: McGuigan's ownership of the gym, his partnership with Toby and Ruben Florio, their piece of Tyrone's contract and those of the other boxers, the date the agreements had been signed. He tried not to look at Tyrone as he went through it, pretending instead to be consulting the pair of Xeroxes Duffy had given him. It took about three minutes.

He finished, pushed the pages across the table, and looked up. Tyrone was glaring at him, his eyes like brands. His upper body was erect, stretched to its limit. He gripped the tabletop on his side with both hands. Harry was suddenly terrified.

"Why you tellin' me this, man? What you tellin' me this for?"

"I thought it was important. I thought you'd want to know."

"How you figure I want to know? What give you the right, man? What give you the right?"

Harry didn't know what to answer. He'd been prepared to be disputed, to be called a liar, even for Tyrone to get up and walk out. But he had no good answer for this.

"You've been lied to. You've been let down. I thought you'd want to know."

Tyrone had stopped looking at him. He was looking nowhere now, slumped backward in the booth, his face a blank. The next thing out of his mouth was almost a mumble.

"You shoulda let it alone, man. Shoulda just let it be."

It came to Harry then. He had known. Or not wanted to know. Or not wanted to be sure.

"I'm sorry. I—"

"You sorry? I don't think you sorry, man. You be pumpin' me for shit since the first day—buyin' me burgers and pumpin', pumpin', pumpin'. So don't be tellin' me now you sorry."

But there was no longer anger in his tone, only flatness. He seemed to have shriveled.

Harry tried to explain. He tried to make him understand why he had done what he had, why he had thought it was the right thing to do. But he saw that Tyrone wasn't hearing him, that he was only throwing out words. Tyrone just sat there, sagged back into the corner of the booth, his shoulders scrunched to half their breadth, his chin now lowered to his chest.

Harry again offered him the Xeroxes—"These are yours if you want them"—but Tyrone just pushed them back at him without a word. It occurred to Harry that he might not know how to read.

The two men sat like that for a few more minutes, neither of them speaking. At some point the waitress arrived, heavyset and jowly, asking would there be anything else. Harry asked for the check. She tore it off her pad, cleared their dishes and retreated.

Harry waited a minute or two more. Still silence. He pulled his coat off the back of the booth and started to stand up, waiting for the other man to follow. Instead he just looked up at Harry from his seat:

"Guess I been a real dumbass, huh?"

Harry sat back down. He reached across the table and put a hand on Tyrone's arm, but the other man pulled away.

"We're all asses sometimes, Tyrone. You want to believe in people. Sometimes they let you down."

Tyrone gave out a small sound, somewhere between a laugh and a grunt.

"*Let you down?* That more than letting you down, man. You trust a guy with your life, he stab you in the back—and you call it *letting you down?*"

"I don't know what I'd call it, Tyrone. I don't even know—"

"I call it *murder.*"

"I'm not sure—"

"He did that, he *murdered* me, man. Same thing, no different . . . I been dead since it happened."

His head shook violently from side to side, his words now in a hoarse whisper.

"*Dead*, man, *dead*! You hear what I'm sayin'? I been dead inside, dead in *here*—" at this he stabbed his chest mercilessly with his fist—"and now you tell me it's been done by my own father? My own *father*, man, same thing . . ."

He slumped back, drained. Harry wished now they had never met.

"I'm sorry, Tyrone." He reached again for his arm and squeezed it. There was no response.

"Maybe you should speak to Toby, tell him how you feel. Maybe he can explain."

"Ain't no explaining now, man. No explaining to be done."

He spoke then in a drone. Harry had to strain to hear him.

"Toby and Ruben—Ruben, my manager—they was together the night of the fight. I seen 'em, talking between rounds. Then Ruben tell me after the second Toby says to dump it. I said he was fulla shit. Ruben says to ask him . . .

"So I do, next day at the gym. Toby says it ain't true, that he wouldn't never do nothin' like that, acted like I was accusing him of murder or something . . ." And here he let out a short laugh.

"I didn't know if I believed him or not. I just didn't want to hear nothing else."

Harry said again that there could be more to it, that he needed to talk with Toby.

"No talking to do now, man. The pretending's over with."

This sounded ominous. "Tyrone, you're not going to *do* anything?"

"*Do* anything? No, man, ain't gonna do nothing . . . Not to Toby anyhow. Couldn't lift a hand against Toby, not if I tried."

"Not to anybody. I need your word on that."

Tyrone paused for a moment, then raised his eyes to look at Harry and muttered:

"Won't do nothin' to nobody. You got my word. Whole lot better than some people's."

"Is there anything I can do, Tyrone?"

"No, man, you done enough. Just go and write your story, or whatever you gonna do."

"The story's not important right now," Harry said. And for that moment he believed it. Then he said something he was surprised to hear himself say.

"You're a good man, Tyrone. You believed in things. You believed in people. Maybe they screwed you over, maybe they didn't. But you believed. That's worth something. It is. It really is."

Tyrone looked back at him dumbly.

"That's *bullshit*, man. What choice you think I had?"

Harry said nothing.

"You shoulda let it be, man. Just let it be."

Then he got up from the table and walked out.

Eighteen

———

Two days later, at a little after four in the morning, the sky over the North Inlet was rent by flames mistaken by some for an early dawn. The first radio reports, brief and sketchy and heard mostly by late-shift casino workers on their way home from work, were on the air by five a.m. Between six and eight they grew more detailed: The fire, it was reported, was under control. Arson was suspected but unconfirmed.

Shortly after eight there were reports of three suspects. By eight-thirty, the wall radio at the mini-mart across from Harry's, where he'd gone for coffee, announced the arrests:

Three local boxers, suspects in this morning's possible arson of The Lucky Lady gym on North Jersey Avenue, have been arrested at the home of one of the suspects and are now in custody, according to police. The gym remains standing, though its interior was reportedly gutted by gasoline bombs thrown by the suspects.

Harry knew right away. For the first minutes, he stood numbly against the closed door of the store's soda cooler, holding his coffee and staring straight ahead. When a customer asked him to move, he did so willingly, then moved back again to his position. There was nothing in his mind. Just cobwebs, just deadness.

He wouldn't remember later returning to his place, or sitting for close to an hour with the phone in his lap, knowing he had to do something, that he couldn't just do nothing. But who to call—the jail? The police? Sarah? Thoughts came to him in a jumble, without chronology or connection: . . . *You shoulda just let it be, man . . . You're in way over your head . . .*

The full story, limp but precise, would run the next morning in the early edition of *The Herald*:

Three local boxers, reportedly angered by rumors of fight fixing, were arrested by police early yesterday after allegedly firebombing the gym in which they trained. The three are being charged on one count each of arson, breaking and entering and criminal trespass and are being held pending arraignment. Bail has been set at $40,000 per man.

All three are local professionals who have fought in casino showrooms. One of the men, Tyrone Everett, 33, of North Vermont Avenue, was once ranked as a middleweight but is currently inactive. The other two, Michael John Biggs, 27, and DeWayne Edwards, 32, both enjoy winning records.

The gym is owned by Victor L. McGuigan of Margate and Philadelphia, a career fight promoter who is active in arranging local bouts, and by two partners, Lee (Toby) Ward, 70, a former welterweight and one-time sole owner of the gym, and Ruben Florio, 65, a local trainer . . .

Harry read it from his desk at *The Herald*. Almost before he had finished, the phone rang. It was Duffy. He didn't trouble himself with hellos.

"Guess you must have told him, huh?"

Harry said that he'd rather not talk about it right then. But Duffy was insistent.

"Listen to me, will you? You gotta stay away from this from now on. No matter what happens—the trial, the sentencing, whatever they do to those guys. Just stay away, don't get anywhere near it. *You hear me, sport?* I'm serious."

"I hear you," Harry said, thanked him for the thought, and hung up.

He thought he might hear from Sarah when she heard the news. He wondered if she'd made the connection. But there was no word. Two days passed, and two nights. The windows in Sarah's condo stayed dark. Early on the third morning, sleepless, Harry called her home number—which he'd sworn never to do. It rang once, then cut to a recording that said it was disconnected.

Nineteen

——

A nd then it was Friday, and Harry's weekend to see Woody, a four-
hour drive north. As much as he usually looked ahead to these
times, he had no heart for it now.

He arrived in late afternoon. Anne and Richard would be away
until Sunday, and Harry had agreed to stay over. Woody was awaiting
him, splayed across the couch in front of the TV, which was tuned to
pro wrestling. He had just come from his Babe Ruth League practice,
and was still in his cleats and uniform. The first game of the season
would be the next day.

Harry joined his son on the couch. They hugged, then did their
four-part, secret-agent handshake, which Harry had taught Woody
when he was two. The sitter, the same sallow-faced matron of two weeks
before, was at the kitchen table, an issue of *Cosmopolitan* opened in
front of her. She greeted Harry with the enthusiasm of a toll collector.

"Mrs. Roberts says to tell you Woody has an ear infection. There's
drops on the counter in the bathroom."

"Thank you, Annette. Did she say what time she'd be back Sunday?"

"Late afternoon."

Harry, who hadn't eaten all day, hacked six inches off the end of a hard salami he'd found in the fridge, then swabbed the diminishing length of meat in a porridge of mayonnaise and hot mustard. From the TV, a voice that called itself The Liquidator vowed in bad English to crush the bones of someone known as Ivan the Hun. The house was wrapped in shadow. Streaks of sunlight like yellow spills crisscrossed the floor. Harry wished now he hadn't agreed to stay over. Though the house was the same one he had shared for four years, he felt already like an intruder.

But the weekend surprised him. Starting with a pancake breakfast the next morning, which they ate at the local Denny's, his son's company was unexpectedly sublime. They talked of small things: the sudden decline of the Red Sox, Woody's team's near-miss as Peewee League hockey champs, the prospect of a fishing trip come June.

Then came the game. Woody batted lead-off, and opened the season with a triple to left field. Harry, from the bleachers, screamed so long and loud he had to remind himself to sit down. His son's next at-bat was a single, followed by a stolen base, which turned into a run when the opposing third baseman let the ball roll through his legs. The team won 10-2.

"I didn't know I could hit that far, Dad," his son said breathlessly, of his triple, as they drove away from the field.

"Isn't it cool to surprise yourself?" Harry said. "Sometimes you think you can't do something till you do it. Then you realize you can, which gives you the confidence to do it again. Maybe even do it *better*."

"Yeah. Next time I want to hit a home run," Woody said.

"Then you probably will."

They went to see *Hoosiers* that night at the local single-screen theater. The movie's heroic inspiration, combined with the lingering effects of that afternoon's triumph, had put Woody in a rare mood. They sat up till eleven talking about legendary heroes, famous long-shot wins, and what it meant to have "grit."

Sunday breakfast was the high point. Harry made waffles and bacon; they sat at the dining table just off the living room, next to a desk with a photo propped, frameless, that Harry had never noticed before. It was of Anne, Richard, Woody, and Richard's daughter, Emma, a pretty blonde-haired girl of about eight whom Harry remembered from the wedding, standing on the porch of what looked to be a hunting lodge or rustic men's club. Richard was a large, handsome man with a narrow face and sharp chin; his hands were resting lightly on the shoulders of the girl, who leaned backward against him, smiling sweetly. On the back, in Anne's careful script, was written, "Northeast Harbor, February '85."

Harry gestured toward the photo, which Woody had seen him staring at.

"So what do you think of him?" he said, as off-handedly as he could manage. He had met Richard only twice, including at the wedding, and had almost no sense of him.

"He's a good guy," Woody said. "I think he's pretty rich. He has his own plane."

"Oh," Harry said.

"But you're more fun. At least most of the time."

Harry said he was glad to hear that. This led, by careful degrees, to an exchange about the trickiness of second marriages, and second fathers. Harry said he thought that sometimes old fathers tried too hard to match what new fathers provided—"presents, trips, all that kinda stuff"—or else they felt bad when they couldn't.

"I know that, Dad," Woody said, with a poor attempt at worldliness. "There's this kid at school who's just like that. His stepdad took him and his mom on this African safari—they saw elephants, lions, zebras, all kinds of stuff. It was all the kid talked about for a month. Plus, his real dad works for a newspaper, like you do. He could never do any of that stuff. I think it's kinda sad."

"What's sad about it?" Harry asked.

"It isn't his real dad's fault that he's not rich."

Harry smiled. "It sounds like you've learned a thing or two about life," he said.

Anne and Richard got back a little after three. They'd been four days in the Bahamas, and had the tans to prove it. They seemed happy together, he thought.

Richard had seen a *60 Minutes* special on Atlantic City, and asked Harry if things there were really as crazy as they sounded. Harry said he hadn't seen the show, but thought they probably were.

"It really does sound like the Wild West down there," Richard said. "I hope you're being careful."

He told Harry that Woody bragged sometimes about "all the stories you write on mobsters and bad guys," and about a press award he'd won recently that Harry didn't remember mentioning to his son.

"He's very proud of you, you know."

Harry didn't know, but it made his day to hear it.

***

He left late Sunday afternoon. For the first two hours of the trip south, from Hartford all the way to the head of the Garden State in Fort Lee, he sang along to sixties oldies on a New York station. When that turned to static near Toms River, he switched over to WAYV, Atlantic City's Top 40 station. At seven o'clock the local news came on, and with it a report on the boxers' upcoming arraignments. With the mention of Tyrone—*a once-ranked middleweight whose allegations of fight fixing have stirred controversy within the boxing community*—Harry felt his mood sink like a stone: He missed Woody. He was missing most of his son's growing-up. Anne seemed happier than he had ever been able to make her. He had been careless with his marriage and his life.

***

It was dark by the time he got home. He poured himself a bourbon and opened a can of Chunky soup. Waiting for it to heat on the stove, he began rummaging through a pair of cardboard boxes in search of a photo his mind had fastened on: of him and Anne, sitting in the open double-door of a Ford van in the summer of 1973, somewhere in Idaho or Montana, hugging and laughing and drunk on Mateus.

He never found the picture, but the image was as clear in his mind as the trip it had been part of: west across the country past the Great Lakes and through the Rockies, in the van with Harry's old mutt, Phoebe, and a pair of air mattresses. The high point of the trip (of their life together, Anne would say later) was three days in a cabin outside Eureka on US 101, living on fried eggs and steamed clams, gawking at the redwoods and listening to the seals at night. Harry had never in his young life been happier, or more hopeful for the future. It seemed an unbridgeable expanse from today.

It was a little past nine. His place had never felt so small. He phoned Woody to say goodnight, but Anne said he was already in bed.

"Asleep already?" Harry said.

"I don't know if he's asleep, but it's too late for him to be talking on the phone—he's got school tomorrow. He had a nice weekend with you, though. He talked all through supper about that big triple he hit. And the stolen base."

Harry felt the tears pooling against the backs of his eyes.

"Yeah, that was pretty cool," he said.

"Are you okay, Harry?"

"I'm fine . . . Listen, Anne, I'm—I'm really sorry about what happened with us."

Her answer was slow to come, but gentle.

"It sounds like you've been drinking, Harry."

They hung up a minute later. Harry switched on the TV to a Philadelphia station—a re-run of *Murder, She Wrote*—and collapsed on the couch in front of it. He was asleep by the time the eleven o'clock news came on:

One of the three men jailed recently for the arson of an Atlantic City gym was reportedly found dead earlier tonight. Police are reporting that Tyrone Everett, a local boxer and city resident, apparently hung himself in his cell sometime after eight o'clock . . .

In the dream he was having, he and Anne were inside the old Ford van, parked on the bank of a river. The sun was shining and the windows were open. Nearby, his mother and Sarah were playing catch with a tennis ball, while Phoebe scampered happily between them.

Twenty

——

S arah was awake by seven that Saturday at Harry's. She declined his offer of breakfast, was sullen and jumpy, and could barely sit still. He gave her back her sneaker, which he'd found in the yard. She thanked him, chugged down half a mug of coffee, then said she had to go.

"What's your hurry?" he asked, though he was pretty sure he knew.

"I just need to get back."

Harry sat down across from her, reached over and took her hand.

"Back to what, Sarah?" he asked, as gently as he could. "Back to your bottle of pills?"

Sarah wrenched her hand free, but Harry grabbed her wrist and held on. She pulled back, but with no more strength than a child. Her teeth were gritted, her head shook from side to side.

"*Fuck you, Harry!* You can't hold me here. You don't own me, you know."

"I don't want to own you. I'd just like to help you if you'll let me."

"Then let me go."

"Sarah, do you remember last night? The stuff you talked about?"

"Yeah, it was all *bullshit*. I made it all up."

"Did you? It didn't sound made up to me."

"What're you, a shrink now?"

Harry looked at her helplessly. He had never seen this person before. "Sometimes I wish I were. It might help me understand you better."

She started to cry. Her lips trembled; her hand shook as she tried to wipe the tears away.

"I'm sorry," she said. "Please, please just let me go."

There was nothing else to do. He said he'd drive her back to her motel.

***

Neither of them said a word in the car. Sarah sat pressed against the passenger-side door, softly crying. Harry tried not to notice. He was angry now, furious at his own helplessness, at the absurd futility of trying to solve this puzzle of a person who would so abase herself in her desperation to be rescued, then—an hour or a day later—seem to want nothing more than to be allowed to self-destruct.

He didn't even know her name. She was Sarah Holmes on her driver's license, but that was a fake and he knew it. Her daughter's surname was Michaelis; there was no telling where that came from, though Sarah had once mentioned that Maryanne had briefly been married. In Atlantic City, her hooker busts had her as Sarah Smith, which was the name she went by when she went by anything at all. Harry guessed that these were only the beginning. He had tried several times to press her, but could never get past the cute jokes she always threw out to waylay him.

Once back from the Ebb Tide, where she had submitted weakly to his hug at her door before ravaging her suitcase to get to her pills, Harry spent the next two hours Googling to find connections. At first all he found was a parade of dreary data. Ripton, New York, where Sarah once told him she'd grown up, was every bit the "dump of a town" she'd said: a population of 420, 96 percent white, 44 percent "economically disadvantaged," 9 percent unemployed, barely half with a high school diploma. The main industries were dairy farming and "social services." The crime rate was twice that of the state. But between 1964 and 1970, the time Harry figured would have spanned Sarah's early school years, there were no homicides or arsons reported.

But the story she had told about her father felt real. Harry searched "Ripton house fires," and was kicked over to the web page of the *Utica News-Press*, the little town's paper of record. There, in a paid search of its archives, Harry found this, dated November 12, 1970:

Ripton resident Desmond Sullivan, 32, a former employee at the Bridgeton Ford plant in Utica, died October 8th in a fire at his residence on Bower Road, according to county officials. The remains of several rags soaked in gasoline were found in the home, say fire investigators, who suspect that Sullivan may have ignited the fire himself then been overcome before he could flee . . .

It all fit. But there was nothing more. Apparently the investigation had ended there. It may have been that Desmond Sullivan had not been widely mourned, Harry thought. Or possibly there was just no follow-up.

But from there it was an easy enough troll through the records. On the New York State sex offender registry, Desmond Patrick Sullivan, born December 20, 1938, was listed as a level-2 risk offender, sentenced in 1967 to thirty six to fifty four months in New York's Upstate Correctional Facility for "deviate sexual intercourse" with an unnamed eleven-year-old female. He had been paroled in February 1969 and was currently listed as deceased.

So there it was. Sarah was Sarah Sullivan, of Ripton, New York: child rape victim, committer of patricide, drug addict, lifelong prostitute, sickly, destitute, mentally unbalanced. A child at sixty years old.

Harry stared at the photo in front of him, of the balding, sallow-faced man who had been her father. It made him want to put his fist through the screen.

***

There was still the question of Uncle Poke. Who was this man who Sarah claimed had raised her from the age of thirteen, who had covered up her crime and protected her secret? She had said he was younger than her father—could he still be alive? And how much of the rest of her story was true? The answers now weren't going to be found online.

Julia arrived from Boston that morning a little after ten o'clock. She hadn't been there five minutes before Harry told her of Sarah's story of the night before—the murdered father, the razed home, Uncle Poke—then of her defiance that morning and her bolt for the bottle of pills. And finally of what he had learned online. He needed to understand, he said, he needed to put it all together.

Fall classes at the college wouldn't start for two more weeks—would she come with him to Ripton? It was a three-hour drive; he promised they'd be back the next day.

Julia listened through it all, without a word, then remained quiet for so long Harry wondered if she might be angry with him for his part in things.

"That might be the saddest story I ever heard," she said finally. "Do you think it's true? Or does she just really need help?"

"I don't know for sure," Harry said. "I guess I think it's true—you had to be there, you had to *see her*. It was like she was in a trance. Then the next thing I know, she's this simpering little kid, asking for a glass of milk. It seemed pretty real to me. And that stuff on the web really bears it out. But I don't know. I've never seen anything like it."

Julia said she'd come with him—"mostly because I want to keep you anchored to reality." But she didn't smile when she said it.

"What do you hope to accomplish with this? Let's say you get the answers you're after—what happens then? Do you confront her with them? What'll that prove? She could just hate you for finding her out."

"Maybe. But if this uncle is still around and I can find him . . . He rescued her once, maybe he would again."

"Maybe he doesn't want to be found. Or she doesn't want to be rescued. You can't know where this is going to lead, Harry. I wish you could just do what you've *been* doing—just being there for her, like you were last night. That's what she needs from you. Not for you to turn into some kind of savior."

***

Almost from the start, Julia had warmed to Sarah. Where Harry had tried—always awkwardly—to be a mentor and provider, Julia was closer to a friend. Part of it, Harry thought, may have had to do with her research at UMass on homeless women, which would have deepened her understanding. But whatever was behind it, she had taken on the relationship with purpose. The two had shopped together, lunched together, occasionally gone on weekend walks by the river. Julia had twice visited Sarah at the hospital. They shared a love of country music and small mongrel dogs, and had once conspired to lure Harry to a kennel and nearly convinced him to adopt one.

And they talked. They talked about almost anything. There was a tenderness between them that Harry loved to see. "You two could be sisters," he had said once to them both.

He was still trying to defend his reasons for the Ripton trip—"This may be our best chance to find out what's behind all this misery"—when Julia cut him off.

"Last night, did she say anything to you about *her daughter?*"

"About Maryanne? No, nothing," he said. "Why would she have? She hardly ever mentions her."

"She does to *me*. Maybe because we both have daughters."

"So what did she say?"

"I'm not supposed to tell you this, but it sounds like you probably should know . . . She told me last week that she hasn't told Maryanne the truth about her father, about who he was. She was in tears over it. It may be part of what's troubling her."

"The race car guy? He died in a crash, right? She said she didn't know him long. I figure he probably started out as a john."

"Kind of like you?"

"I guess so, yeah. Except I'm still around."

"This guy could be, too," Julia said. "At least from what Sarah tells me."

"So who was he?"

"She wouldn't say. It's like this dark secret she's carrying around. She seems kind of tortured by it."

"She seems pretty tortured in general lately," Harry said. "It's hard to know the difference with her between what's real and what's not."

Twenty-One

————

Mарch turned to April. The air, no longer wintry though not
yet quite warm, swept off the beach in salty blusters, slapping
against the glass fronts of the Boardwalk casinos, swirling flags and
rattling windows. The sweet, wet, promissory air of a beach town in
springtime—vaguely fishy, as wholesome as new bread.

The Boardwalk, nearly lifeless until a week before, was now a con-
course of retirees. They were the season's first harbinger: local couples
mostly, from Ventnor or Margate, in their late sixties and seventies,
swaddled under car coats, the men in homburgs and shiny leather
gloves, the women in bright hats—walking arm in arm, taking the air.
They stooped against the wind but seldom slowed their pace, and rarely
talked while walking, a purposeful, familiar silence. Their dogged ele-
gance recalled to Harry a disused term: promenade.

From a wooden booth in a sandwich shop just downbeach from
Resorts, he watched them pass, studying the faces. He had always
been intrigued by the couples. Once he had devoted a column to
them for the paper, in which he wrote that as long as they kept returning to the Boardwalk every April—like the swallows to Capistrano,

he wrote—the city would still retain a piece of its soul, however small. But that when they stopped coming, when they no longer survived to come, it would be a sign that the past was dead and the city was as cold and barren as the Boardwalk in winter. It was an extravagant image, but it held some truth for him.

The restaurant smelled, as always, of Mazola oil and stale heat. It used to be Harry's favorite on the Boardwalk: a glitz-less, open-fronted, pre-casino place, one of the few left in the city, with dark wood booths slathered in tourist graffiti ("Bill and Maureen in Love, Lisle, Illinois"). Smeared color glossies—the owner with Bill Cosby, pretty blondes in T-shirts biting into fried chicken—hung at odd angles on the walls, Motown blared from corner speakers. The food was cheap but decent, the coffee was always fresh and breakfast was served till closing. Except in summer, it was rarely crowded, and even then you could sit half the day over bagels and coffee.

It was the end of the day. The sun was yielding by degrees to the yellow neon of casino marquees. There were fewer couples now. Most of those still out were walking westward, on return legs to condos or tidy single-families on Georgia or Tallahassee Avenues, where—Harry had once written in a column—"they will sip gin from old stemware, draw baths and watch the news on TV. The men will read the financial pages; the women will phone their daughters."

Harry envied them.

***

He was there for Sarah. The afternoon before, unable to work, at times even to think straight—it had been that way often since the news of Tyrone—he had come home early from *The Herald* to find her message on his phone. It was the first time he'd heard her voice in more than a year and a half. The sound of it, in those first moments, sent such a tremor through him he could barely register what she said:

Harry, I need to see you. It's important. There's a place called Dipstix, on the Boardwalk. It's a tourist place, you probably know it. I'll meet you there tomorrow at four. Please, Harry, it's important. I need to talk to you.

He didn't recognize her, even after she sat down. She wore a brown leather jacket over a purple T-shirt whose front read "Life's A Beach." Her hair was blonde now, pulled straight back and streaked with green; she wore grungy black jeans torn at the knees; her breasts were cinched in. Her lips were black. She'd turned herself into an androgynous punk.

"*Jesus*," Harry said.

"Yeah, I know. I'm pretty good at disguises."

She sat down and pulled a pack of Newports from her purse.

"I didn't know you smoked."

"I do now."

"So who're you hiding from?"

"Everyone. The world. Anyone who'd know me. Listen, Harry, I didn't come here to talk about my looks."

"Okay. But I don't want to talk about Tyrone."

"I don't either. It's too awful to even think about. That's not why I wanted to see you."

Harry tried to think clearly, but the thoughts wouldn't come. Everything seemed suddenly too big. Tyrone dead, the old Sarah gone, this new, punk Sarah with her black lips and new resoluteness. He felt delirious.

"So why?"

She lit the cigarette and exhaled almost fiercely.

"They want to kill you."

"So you came here to warn me?"

"*Why, Harry? Why'd you tell him that stuff?*"

He was stunned, but not surprised. "How do you know what I told him?"

"Never mind how I know. Why did you tell him?"

He answered with the only answer he knew—the same one he'd been answering to himself for the past ten days.

"I thought he had a right to know. It's *his* life. I never thought he'd—"

"So now you're going to write it for the paper?"

"I don't know. I might. I think he would have wanted me to."

"They'll kill you if you do." She said it flatly, factually.

"Why don't they just kill me anyway?"

"I think they figure you're not the only one at the paper who knows about that stuff, that somebody else would still write the story. Then if you were dead already, there'd be a connection."

"And if I write it myself?"

"They'll probably wait a while, but sooner or later they'll get you."

"Is that what they told you?"

"They didn't tell me anything. I'm gone from them, I'm done, finished—that's why I look like this, so they won't find me. I just know how they are, that's what they do."

But Harry was somewhere else now.

"I've missed you," he said. "I think of you a lot."

Sarah just stared at him. "Harry, do you understand what I'm telling you?"

"Do you remember that old inn we went to in Cape May? The one with the old guy on the beach?"

She glanced at him quickly, then turned away.

"I was there one night last week. The place is closed down, boarded up. Looks like it's out of business."

"What were you doing there?"

"Nothing. Just looking at the beach and remembering that night."

Sarah dropped her head and put her hand to her face. When she spoke again, there was anger in her voice.

"*Harry, are you listening?* If you write that story they're gonna kill you. You're gonna be *dead*. Do you get that?"

"So that's what you came here to tell me?"

"Yes. But not only that."

"What else, then?"

Sarah leaned over the table, looked at him, blew out another lung-ful of smoke and shook her head.

"There's going be a trial. The two other boxers who torched the place, they're gonna be tried."

"I know that."

"I want to be a witness. I want to try to get them off."

For a long time, he said nothing. Then the fog began to part.

"What are you talking about? They *did it*, they burned the place down. There's no case."

"You remember what I told you about, that night with those guys on the houseboat?"

"What about it?"

"They were all really drunk, they were mouthing off. The boxer I was with, he was the one who was supposed to beat Tyrone in that fight at Resorts. He kept talking about that, about how it had been set up for him to win, and he was going to make it big after that—but Tyrone had messed it all up, he kept punching when his trainer told him to quit."

"*Castillo? Esteban Castillo?*" That's the creep who beat you up that night?"

"Yes, but that's not what I'm talking about. I'm talking about the fixing, about Vic McGuigan and all the fixing. That's why those guys burned the gym. It's why Tyrone is dead. I'm going to tell about it."

"Who'll believe you?"

"They'll believe me. There were other fights too. I know about some of it. I know other stuff too."

Harry said nothing.

"I've seen a lawyer. I've told her things. She said she'd represent those two guys. So it'll all be in court, it'll be public. Anyway, it's what I'm going to do."

"Who's this lawyer? Who's paying for her?"

"I have money saved. Her name's Adele Russo. She's from Philly."

Harry felt flattened. It was all too much.

"You warn *me* not to write a story, and you're going to *testify* against them? Are you out of your mind, Sarah?"

For the first time, Sarah smiled, the same sad little smile Harry had so loved. His thoughts went back to that day at her place, with Tyrone and the roses, the day that everything started. It occurred to him that perhaps her whole life had led up to this.

"There are ways to testify without being in court. I've talked to the lawyer about it."

"So you'll still be in hiding?"

"Yeah, I guess I'll be '*in hiding*'—that makes it sound way too weird. Anyway, I don't think they'll find me."

They talked until the sun was almost gone. It was getting cold, the kitchen had closed, the staff was sweeping up. Sarah would say nothing of how she had left her place or parted from Touch of Class, or of where she was living. Only that she was "around," and that she had enough cash to get by.

They walked outside onto the Boardwalk. There was a cool wind blowing off the ocean. Sarah pulled up the collar of her leather jacket and zipped it halfway up. Harry put his arm around her as they walked. He felt his balance returning.

"*So will you please not write the story?*"

"I don't know. It's an important story. And I feel like I kind of owe that to Tyrone."

Sarah jerked herself free and walked to the railing, where she turned and faced him. She looked close to tears.

"*Can't you please try to understand?* Nothing you write is going to make any difference. You can't help Tyrone, he's *dead*. And I don't want you to die too; I *really* don't want you to die."

Harry went to her, took her in his arms and began to rock her gently. It was all he'd wanted to do since she'd arrived. He was almost happy now.

"Okay. I won't write it."

He felt Sarah's shoulders sag. "I'm glad," she said. "It's the right thing."

"How about you? When all this is over, are you going to get out of here?"

"Please, Harry—"

"It's what *I'm* going to do," Harry said—a decision he'd made in that moment. "As soon as I can. I'm going to finish up at *The Herald*, give my notice and get out. I can't stand it anymore."

"Well, good, I'm glad. Get as far away as you can."

"You could come with me. "

"I can't do that."

"You can't or you won't?"

Sarah shook her head, took a long breath, then let it out.

"There are things you don't know. Please, Harry, don't ask me to explain."

It was the same old story—never any questions. Harry said nothing, instead wrapped his arms around her, pressing her into the railing. She smiled, raised her arms and put them around his waist.

"This is where I kiss you," he said.

"Okay."

And he did. Unsurely at first—it had been such a long time—until her arms tightened around him and he felt some of that wonderful, trembling urgency he remembered.

"I've missed you," he said.

"Me too."

"Can we go somewhere?"

Sarah shook her head slowly. "I need to go."

For a long time neither of them spoke. They just closed their eyes and held each other, Sarah's face buried in the weave of Harry's sweater. An older couple shuffled past, the last stragglers of the early-evening promenaders. The air was turning colder—street lamps and neon were the only light left.

"I love you," Harry said.

Sarah put her index finger to her mouth and made a quiet *shhhhh*. "Let's not say those things," she whispered.

"But I do."

"I've got to go now," she said.

"When will I see you again?"

"I don't know."

Then she turned and walked quickly away. Harry watched till she turned left off the Boardwalk, then down the stairs to the street.

Twenty-Two

———

August 2017

The town of Ripton was much as he'd imagined. A rutted main street less than 200 yards long, running down the center with a scattering of alleyways fish-boned off it on both sides. The heart of the town seemed to be the Ripton IGA, a barn-size wood place painted in a fading yellow, with several cars parked outside. There was also Ripton Hardware, the Ripton Diner, Crofty's Bait and Tackle, Walt's Taxidermy, Frenchy's Liquors, a laundromat with three washers, a two-pump Shell station and a small but tidy Methodist church. None of them appeared prosperous. Several were in need of new roofs. At the far end of town stood the burnt-out remains of what had once been the Slumber Inn Motel. For Harry, it was like driving through a giant, live diorama that might be called The End of Hope.

On a side alley off the main street, they found the town's one-room library, which shared the second floor of the two-story Ripton Town Hall, one of the few brick buildings in the town. *"Open Wednesday through Sunday noon to 6:00,"* the neatly hand-printed sign on the door read. Harry and Julia went in together.

The room's only occupant, an ancient-looking, elegant woman in a blue silk blouse—Harry guessed she must be close to ninety—sat behind a small desk in front of the library's card cabinet, an elaborately carved cane next to her on the desk. A collection of mismatched wooden bookshelves lined three walls. On a table in the center, facing each other, were two vintage PCs.

The woman's name was Mrs. Bohannan. Harry introduced himself and Julia, relating their purpose there as truthfully as possible: He had an old friend who was unwell and now suffering from a kind of dementia; she had once mentioned that she had family in the area, but could no longer recall more than that. It had been a long time.

"Oh dear, that seems to be happening to so very many people nowadays," Mrs. Bahaman said, in a crisp, very proper voice. "It's tragic for the families, isn't it? I'm so blessed to still have my wits about me . . . So tell me, what is your friend's name?"

"Sarah," Harry said. "Sarah Sullivan."

The woman smiled broadly, her face crinkling like a sheet of onion skin.

"Oh my, yes, Sullivan. There used to be *so many* Sullivans in Ripton. And in Bridesport, too, the next town over. They used to say, if you met a man in the street and couldn't remember his name, you'd best just call him Mister Sullivan."

The old woman chuckled, then looked up at Harry from her seat at the desk.

"But that hasn't been true for a long while."

"What happened?" Harry asked. Did they all leave town?"

"Oh, you know how it is," the woman said. "A few moved on, a few died, the young people couldn't leave soon enough. There isn't much to keep people here anymore, I'm afraid."

The three of them chatted for a few minutes about the lure of cities, the lack of opportunity in small towns—Julia citing her own early experience as a "born-and-bred small town girl"—before Harry asked if Sarah's name rang any bells.

"I don't know," the woman replied. "As I said, there were so many Sullivans. How long ago would she have left?"

"Probably around the early seventies," Harry said. "Maybe even sooner. She was just a kid."

"A long time ago. Do you know the name of her mother or father?"

"I think her father's name might have been Desmond."

The woman looked down at her hands, then up at Harry, then at Julia. She shook her head slowly.

"That was a very sad story," she said.

"Yes, I think I know some of it," Harry said. There are records."

The woman didn't answer. She sat, still shaking her head, lost in thought now. It seemed she had nothing more to say. Close to a minute went by before Harry broke the silence.

"Do you remember anything at all about Sarah? Desmond's daughter?"

The woman looked up at him. "You say she's lost her memory, this Sarah?"

"A lot of it, yes. She's confused about things."

"Well then, that's a mercy, I suppose," the woman said.

Harry was unsure how to go forward, and was about to ask if there might be someone else in town who could help him, when the woman raised her head and looked at him through squinted eyes.

"Do you know about *the uncle?*"

"Sarah did mention an uncle. She didn't say who he was."

"A *monster*," the woman said.

"I didn't know that," Harry said. "Sarah never said much about him, except that he took her in when her father died."

The woman's look had turned to a glare.

"Oh yes, *he took her in*, all right! He most certainly *took her in*. He took in lots of people. He was a very smart man, smart and handsome and as cunning as a fox . . . And that's all I have to say about it."

The woman was plainly shaken. "I'm sorry, but I can't talk any more about this, it's too upsetting. Vince Sullivan was a *monster*, a stain on this town, he and his brother both. You should hope your friend never hears his name again."

"I understand," Harry said. "His name was Vince, you said?"

"Yes, Vince. And whatever else he called himself. It's nearly five o'clock. I'm going home now." At that, she took hold of her cane and stood up slowly.

"If you want to know more, you can read it in the paper."

"The paper?" Harry said. "I checked the Utica paper and couldn't find anything."

"Not *Utica*," the woman said, her voice oozing disdain, as she made her way now slowly toward the door. "That paper never reports anything worthwhile. It was our own little paper—it covered Ripton, Paintsville, and Bridesport. It's been gone for years now, but it used to come out monthly. There was an article in there about all this. I know, because it was my son who wrote it."

"I'd like very much to read it," Harry said.

"We have all the back issues here. But I'm closing up now. If you want to see it you'll have to come back tomorrow. We open at noon."

✳✳✳

Harry didn't have a number for Desmond Sullivan's old house on Bower Road. But the road, when he found it, was less than fifty yards long, and there were only five houses on it, one of them abandoned, another with a wheelless old junker in the yard. At the far end was an empty lot, choked in weeds, the blackened remains of a stone chimney at its center. It was here, Harry guessed, that Sarah had suffered through her early years.

He stopped the car and stared out. "Can you imagine growing up here?" he said. Julia didn't answer. For the next five minutes they sat silently and looked out across the road. Then they drove away.

They spent that night at the Super 8 in Bridesport, the only motel between Ripton and the interstate, according to GPS. Neither one was in a mood for talking. They watched a show on the Nature Channel they would forget by morning. "Thanks for coming with me," Harry whispered to Julia after he turned out the light. "I'm really glad you're here." He reached out his hand and stroked her hair, then pulled himself closer and kissed her. The kiss she returned was lifeless.

"I can't right now, Harry, I'm sorry. All I can think of is the two of them, in that miserable little hovel all those years. It's just so sick. And so sad. It's like something out of a Gothic novel. Only worse."

***

They were back at the library a little after noon on Sunday, a few minutes behind Mrs. Bohannon. The March 1972 issue of *The Tri-Town Reporter* was awaiting them on the computer table, turned to page three, where the story, "Bridesport Man Arrested in Underage Prostitution Sting" ran under the photo of a burly, snappily dressed man pictured with his lawyer outside a Utica courthouse:

A local man, Vincent Sullivan, 29, faces charges of sex trafficking and soliciting a child for prostitution after allegedly recruiting an underage victim to work in Utica as a prostitute, law enforcement sources say. The female juvenile, according to reports, initially approached an undercover detective on the night of February 24th on West Street in the vicinity of the River City Motel, where she entered his car and offered him oral sex in exchange for $50. The victim reportedly told the detective that Sullivan had offered her jewelry, luxury clothing and large amounts of money in exchange for her services. Sullivan, a Bridesport native, is the manager of All-Star Boxing, a Utica training gym . . .

Harry felt himself freeze. He looked again at the photo of the man with his lawyer. He wasn't familiar, just a street hood in a fancy suit, the kind you see every day in any courtroom. But the picture was more than forty years old.

There was no follow-up story in the paper's files about the outcome of the case. A Google search for "Vincent Sullivan Utica" turned up two other references between 1973 and '77. The first was a quote from Sullivan about a property dispute, the other a short item about the arrest of a boxer who had reportedly attacked him with a knife. And after that, nothing. A property search showed that the gym had closed in 1978.

Harry took a photo on his phone of the news story, another of the picture. Then he walked over to where Julia was sitting on a bench by the front door, and showed her the phone. She read the story slowly, then scrolled back and seemed about to read it again.

"*Jesus,*" she said. "Do you think it was her?"

"It looks like it," Harry said. "He burns down the house in November of 'seventy, Sarah moves in with him—she's what then, thirteen, fourteen? Then two years later he's pimping an underage kid in a city ten miles away? I'd be surprised if it wasn't her."

Julia looked up at him from the bench. "Harry, are you sure you want to keep going with this?"

But Harry had barely heard her. He walked over to Mrs. Bohannan, who was tagging books at her desk. He thanked her very much for her help before he asked his question.

"About Vince Sullivan—as far as you know, did he go to prison on those charges?"

The older woman looked up from her work and stared at him coldly.

"No, he didn't go to prison. That lawyer of his put that poor child on the stand and turned her into *a liar*, just tore her apart, tore her to pieces. They say she was in tears by the end. *A child!*—can you imagine?"

"No, I can't. That's awful. So they found him not guilty?"

"Yes, they found him not guilty. And he and the girl just walked out and *disappeared*! They let him just walk away with her, after all that monster had done. . . . God help her, is all I can say."

"And I guess no one knows where they went from here?" Harry knew he was pressing, but he couldn't let it go.

"I have no idea. No one around here has seen him in years. A good thing, too."

Harry thanked the woman and turned to go, but she wasn't finished.

"I did hear a while ago, it must be ten years ago now, that someone saw him in Utica, that he had come back and was in some sort of home there. But that was just a rumor going around."

Harry opened his mouth to say something more when he felt Julia, beside him now, her elbow in his side.

"You've been *so* helpful Mrs. Bohannan," she said to the woman. "Thank you for being so generous with your time."

She put her arm through Harry's, and began guiding him toward the door. He stopped midway. "There's one more thing I need to check," he said, and moved toward the computer table. "It won't take long."

Julia just nodded. "I'll wait in the car," she said.

***

Twenty minutes later, a little after one o'clock, they sat across from each other in a Wendy's just north of Ripton, drinking lemonades and sharing a sandwich. Other than their orders, neither one had spoken since they arrived.

"So what did you find?" Julia said finally. She seemed tired.

"First I need to tell you something," Harry said. Julia put down her drink and waited.

And he told her the whole story, all the way back: about Vic

McGuigan, the boxers, the houseboat, the gym fire, the mob connections. It was the first time in more than thirty years he'd told anyone. Then he told her what he was thinking.

"He'd be about the right age. Mid-seventies, maybe eighty. They both trained fighters, they were both pimps. Sullivan's gym here closed down in 'seventy-eight, the same year the first casino opened in AC—pro boxing was big there from the start, just like in Vegas. He may have brought some fighters with him, or just sold himself as a trainer, I don't know. He was a pretty slick guy."

Julia hadn't said a word. She seemed stunned, her fist clenched against her upper teeth.

"Somewhere along the line he might have had to change his name. If he had any kind of record, the Commission in AC wouldn't have let his boxers fight in the casinos."

"Did the picture look like him?"

"I couldn't tell. That photo was ancient, and I never met McGuigan personally, just saw him from a distance a couple of times. But they're both about the same size and they both had light hair. I don't know, it all kind of lines up. Either that, or it's just a really wild coincidence."

"And this would be her actual uncle, right?"

"Right, Uncle Poke, her father's brother. It's a nickname Sarah says people gave him. Apparently the guy was always talking about all the women he'd like to 'poke.' So that's what they called him."

Julia grimaced, then shook her head. "So tell me the rest of it. What did you find when you went back?"

"According to Address Dot Com, there's a Vincent Sullivan at a place called Saint Anthony's Haven, on Pembroke Street in Utica. It's half an hour away."

"My God."

"Will you come with me? I just want to see the guy, that's all. I'm pretty sure I'll know if it's him."

Julia's eyes narrowed. She looked away, then back.

"Of course I'll come with you. How could I not? But I *hate* this whole thing, Harry. I really hate it."

"So do I," Harry said. "But I think we're almost there."

Twenty-Three

———

Tyrone "the Cyclone" Everett was no more. The whole North Inlet seemed to be mourning him. At the memorial service they held a month after he died, at the little park outside the Christian Fellowship Church on a gray morning that threatened rain, nearly a hundred people took seats on the grass and on the benches with more on the street outside. It was as though he had been the mayor, or a preacher, or the champion of something. More than a dozen people stood up to speak—boxers, elders, childhood friends, a homeless man who spoke of his kindness and called him a saint. Eel, the young boxer Tyrone had sparred with, fighting tears all the way through his short speech, called him "the big brother I always wanted." Toby, who seemed to have organized the gathering, told stories from Tyrone's boyhood, spoke of his bravery in Vietnam, his "little kid" playfulness and his "beautiful closeness" to his mother, who was present in a wheelchair, despite her illness, though she would die a month later. "I loved him like a son," Toby said. "Sometimes it was hard to remember that he wasn't one."

Harry, one of the few white people in the crowd, watched it all from his spot on the grass. He looked for any sign of Sarah—it occurred to him she might show up in one of her disguises—but she hadn't come. He didn't know where she was or how to reach her.

As the crowd began to break up, he remained sitting, still at his place on the grass. Eel, fully in tears by now, approached and sat along-side. Harry felt a sudden tenderness toward the boy, who today in his street clothes looked no older than sixteen. He wrapped an arm around his shoulder. Eel seemed comforted by this, which brought some com-fort to Harry. So for several minutes the pair sat without speaking as the crowd dispersed around them.

"He ain't coming back," the boy said finally. "He gone, and he ain't never coming back."

Harry said nothing, just tightened his grip around the boy in reply.

"He was good to me, he cared about me. Like I said, just like my big brother, no different." And at this, his shoulders shook harder and he buried his head in his hands.

"He was a good man," Harry said. "I didn't know him nearly as long as you did, but I liked him a lot. I wanted to help him. I wish he hadn't done what he did."

Eel's head jerked up as though he'd been shocked.

"You mean *kill hisself*? No way he kill hisself, no way!"

"I just know that's what the police reported," Harry said quietly.

"The police is *lying*! They *lying*! There ain't no way he killed hisself! DeWayne was there, *he knew*! We went to the jail afterwards, to see him and Mikey, and he told us hisself!"

"Told you what?"

"DeWayne and Mikey and Tyrone was all there together, the three of them, their cells all in a row, like. Then that night the cops come down and take Tyrone away, they take him away separate, and he don't come back. The next morning they tell people he done hanged hisself in his cell. They say they took him to a different cell to talk, and they left and he hanged hisself. *They lying! Somebody lying!* Somebody done *lynched him* that night!"

Harry said nothing, and Eel went on talking. He talked about how Tyrone had been cheated out of a win and maybe a shot at the title someday, and how he had planned to "tell his story" at the trial. He talked about handlers and trainers he said he knew were crooked, and about a boxer named Floyd he claimed had his fingers broken the year before when he threatened to spread the word on some fix. He never mentioned McGuigan by name, or mentioned Toby. Mostly he rambled and he wept. The longer he went on, the less weight Harry put on anything he said—except the parts about Tyrone being taken from his cell, and about his plan to tell his story.

"What was he going to tell about?" he asked when Eel finally fell silent.

"All of it. All that bad shit that happened to him, about how they screwed him, he was gonna tell all of it. He coulda won the title someday."

"What about DeWayne? Is he planning to say something at the trial?"

"I dunno. He didn't say nothin' about that. Mostly he was jus' talkin' about Tyrone. He might, though. I dunno, but he might."

The boy was quiet then, crying softly into the sleeve of his gray Caesars sweatshirt. It had begun to rain. Around them, the park had emptied.

"Where are you headed now?" Harry asked.

"Home, I guess," the boy said. "Ain't nowhere else to go. Ain't no gym to go to no more."

Harry walked with him the three blocks to his mother's home on Baltic Avenue, hugged him at the door and promised to stay in touch.

***

It was nearly six o'clock, and raining harder, by the time he got back to his car. It would be night soon. Harry had no one to see and nowhere to go, except back to his three-room place in Chelsea, which felt more and more like a prison. He thought of Eel, a boy of eighteen who had just lost his hero. He wondered what would become of him; maybe one of the older boxers would take him under his wing—but how could that happen with the gym gone? He thought of Sarah, and wondered where she was. The last he'd seen her was at Dipstix, the day she told him about the lawyer she'd hired, more than three weeks ago now. He thought the plan was crazy. He hoped she'd given it up.

He had just gotten in his car when he saw a man in his fifties, paunchy, in a dark blue suit, with an oversized umbrella he was struggling to open—emerge from the car in front of him. Harry watched as the man tussled with the umbrella, then seemed to give up. Instead, he walked quickly to the passenger's side of Harry's car and began rapping on the window with his free hand, shouting to be heard.

"*Mister Hopper, Mister Hopper!*—can you let me in? I got somethin' to tell you!"

Harry reached across and opened the door. The man got in.

"Wet out there!" he said. He was sitting now in the seat next to Harry, the collapsed umbrella dribbling a slow puddle at his feet. He was pudgy all over, with pale skin, close-cropped gray hair and a head shaped like a giant bell pepper. He seemed out of breath from his struggle with the umbrella and his scamper between cars.

"What do you want?"

"My name's Wynn," the man said. "Lennie Wynn. I work for Vic McGuigan."

Harry felt the muscles in his shoulders go taut.

The man offered his hand, which Harry took, pumped once and released.

"What do you want?" he asked again.

"We met once, long time ago. You was writing a story. I used to manage singers."

Harry didn't recall, but nodded anyway. "So what do you want to tell me?"

"Well first, that was a real nice service they did for the boxer. Real nice. It's a shame what happened to him. Looks like he really broke some hearts, too. His mama 'specially—did you see her sitting there in that chair, crying her eyes out? Poor woman. I really feel for her, I do."

"What do you want, Wynn?"

Harry was angry now, and frightened, though he tried not to show it. He had a powerful sense, as dumb and useless as this man seemed, that there was trouble coming.

"The boxers. They been let out."

"What do you mean, 'let out'? Let out of jail?"

"Yeah. Toby came and got 'em. They was like his kids, you know. Just like he said at the service—not just the Everett guy, all of 'em. They all like his kids. So he came and got 'em out."

"What about the charges?" Harry was stupefied now, almost speechless.

"Shouldnt'a *been* no charges. That was a misunderstanding, is all. Buncha dirty old rags in the back, just caught fire and burnt. Happens all the time, that's what the fire marshal says."

"That's not what he said then."

"Made a mistake, I guess," the man said.

Harry's impotence hit him like a voltage surge. His cheeks were burning. The muscles in his jaw worked against each other like jammed pistons.

"Is there *anybody* you guys can't buy? Anybody at all? You make me *sick*, you know that?"

"Don't do that, Mister Hopper, don't be getting sick on me. There's more I got to tell you."

Harry was quiet, breathing deeply now against the anger in his chest.

"I don't know why you're so upset," the man said. "I heard about that lawyer your girlfriend got. Seems to me like you guys are off the hook. Those legal bills would have been a real bitch."

The man smiled narrowly behind thick lips. "Mind if I smoke?"

He pulled a pack from his shirt pocket and stabbed a cigarette crudely into the precise center of his mouth. There was a small click as it tapped his middle teeth, which were faintly yellow. He pushed in the car lighter, withdrew it slowly and lit the cigarette, then took a long drag and exhaled a cloud of smoke.

"A real bitch," he said again. "I bet she had to put up some bucks already, huh? Those lawyers, they want it in advance, won't trust you for nothin'. . . Probably won't give her back none of it now either, now that there won't be no trial. Not all of it, anyway. Seems a shame, is all."

The man pulled a thick white envelope from his suitcoat pocket, tapped it twice against his knee, then rested it carefully on the seat between them. "Vic and the others, Toby too, they thought it'd be good if you and her was reimbursed. All that time and trouble, not to mention the advance money."

Harry's eyes fixed on the envelope as though it were a weapon.

"Good for *who?*" he said.

"For everybody. For you, for everybody . . . Vic and the others, they don't like all this talk about fixin' fights and all. That's real bullshit talk. Long time ago, they usta fix fights. Can't do it no more, with the Commission and all. Don't pay anyway—too much money in the purses."

"Cut the shit, Wynn."

"I know what Everett told you about Toby and all, and the dive he was s'posed to take. A misunderstanding's all it was."

Harry was seething now. "You try to buy him too? Before you strung him up?"

The man broke into a false, staccato laugh.

"What you talkin' about? Nobody's stringing up nobody. You seen too many shitty movies, Harry. And you keep talking about' *buy*' . . . '*buy*,' '*buy*,' '*buy*.' Why you tryin' to bust my balls, Harry?—you don't mind if I call you that? Vic don't buy nobody. Nobody, ever. He's a rich man, and he can buy what he wants, but he don't buy *people*. People ain't for sale, Harry, you ought to know that."

"So why the envelope?"

"Like I told you, *reimbursement*. Time and trouble. And money. That's all. You don't want it, don't take it. No big thing. Just don't be bustin' my balls, okay?"

"I don't want it."

"No problem." The man returned the envelope, with minor ceremony, to his jacket pocket.

"Like I say, Harry, this bullshit about fixin' fights—well, that's what it is, a crock 'a shit. Edwards and the other guy, they're straight on that now. How about you? You straight on it too, Harry?"

"I didn't take your money, asshole. I'm straight on *nothing*."

There was a pause. The man scratched his crotch, then leaned back heavily in his seat.

"You oughtta call me Lennie, my name's Lennie . . . You know, that lady you hang around with, that Sarah, she's a real sweetheart, an honest-to-god sweetheart. I envy you, I do . . . I hear, though, she gets depressed a lot, takes pills and stuff? I hope to hell you can keep her from doin' that, a woman like her shouldn't be doin' that to herself."

Harry lunged. Before the man had time to flinch, he had him by the necktie, his knuckles squeezing upward into his windpipe, bending his head backward into the seat top. The man struggled briefly, then stopped, his eyes as wide as half-dollars.

"You're breakin' my neck!"

"Get the fuck outta my car, Wynn! Get the fuck out!"

He released him. The man's head bobbed forward like a spring, the cigarette still between his fingers. He stabbed it out in the ashtray without looking up, then threw open the door. He was halfway out before he opened his mouth to speak.

"That was dumb, Harry. For such a smart guy, you're pretty fuckin' dumb."

"Don't forget your umbrella, Wynn!"

Harry flung the umbrella straight-armed from the seat, watched it land in a puddle a dozen feet away, slammed the door and put the car in gear. He hadn't a clue where he was going. If he were shaking any harder, it would have been useless to decide.

Twenty-Four

———

August 2017

It was a plain, single-story brick building on a side street, whose sole flourishes were a small red awning and a bed of daylilies outside. Once inside, the only person in sight, behind a counter at the entrance, was a stout, middle-aged woman with pixie-cut graying hair, a kind face, and a paper name tag that asked "How Can I Help?" Julia had offered to do the honors, which she did with a smile.

"Good afternoon. We're here to visit Vince Sullivan. I hope this is a good time?"

"Of course. Every day till seven. Are you family?"

"No. We're friends of his niece, Sarah Sullivan. She couldn't come herself, but asked that we visit when we were in town."

The woman looked briefly confused, then repeated what she'd heard, squeezed herself out from behind the counter and trundled off down a short hallway. Harry could feel his heart pounding.

She was only gone a minute or two. She returned looking troubled.

"How long has it been since his niece visited?" she asked.

"I don't know for sure, I know it's been a while," Julia said. "She lives kind of far away."

"Then she may not have told you what to expect."

"Nothing special, no. Is there a concern?"

"Oh no, no concern. Just that Mister Sullivan is an old man, that's all, he can get a little crotchety. He's not used to getting visitors—I've been here over a year now, and you all are the first I've seen. . . . He's one of our quieter guests, doesn't mingle a lot, just stays in his room and reads his boxing magazines. Did you know he used to be a boxer?"

"A trainer, actually," Harry said. It was the first time he'd spoken.

"Oh, a trainer. Yes, I think maybe that is what he said. I hardly know the difference myself. But he's a nice enough man. Just getting on, is all, like most of our guests." And the woman smiled warmly. "But he'll be happy to see you, I'm sure."

*

The man sat alone in a wheelchair facing the open door, in a small bedroom a few yards from where they'd been talking. He was hunched over from the waist, his head only inches above his knees, which were together, his legs splayed beneath them in an inverted V. He arched his neck up when he heard them enter, which caused his mouth to gape open, but his shoulders remained slumped. His face was sickly pale and seemed somehow made of misfitted parts, everything too big or too small. He had no cheeks at all, just sunken expanses. What teeth he had were yellow. An uneven gray stubble covered his face and most of his head. Only his eyes seemed alive, and they were fixed like tiny lasers on Julia.

"*You're not Sarah,*" he said, in a voice so gravelly from disuse it sounded as though it must be painful to use.

"No, sir, I'm not. My name is Julia, and this is my friend Harry. We're friends of Sarah's. She couldn't come herself, so she asked us to stop in on you."

"Couldn't come herself, huh? Sick or locked up, or just didn't want to make the trip—which is it?" It was hard to tell if this was meant as a slur or as some kind of humor.

Julia paused, then answered quietly. "She hasn't been well lately, Mister Sullivan, but maybe she can come another time."

This answer seemed to settle him. He grunted and swiveled his head in the direction of Harry.

"And who're you, buddy?"

Harry said he was also a friend of Sarah's.

"Seems like she has a lot of friends. Well, that's good, she oughtta. She's a good girl, always was a good girl." Then he paused and seemed to be trying to think or to remember something.

"What did she say about me?"

Neither of them answered. The old man waited, then answered for them.

"I'm the only family she has, you know. I raised her from when her daddy died."

Julia nodded. "Yes, that's what she said."

"Damn straight I raised her. Paid the bills, saw her through school, raised her like my own kid. And I trained boxers, too. Did you know that? Middleweights mostly, that was my specialty. I trained some big ones, too . . ."

"Did you really?" Harry cut in now. "Here in Utica? I'm a fight fan myself. I never knew Utica was much of a boxing town."

The man paused, but only briefly. "No, no, not just here. I trained 'em all over—Philly, New York, Jersey, all over. Had some big ones, too—there was one, Archie Johnson, reached Number Six, a real mauler. Would have had a shot at Number One, but then he got hit with a liver punch in his next to last bout, wasn't worth a damn after that."

"Archie Johnson, yeah, I remember him," Harry said, working to measure himself, knowing now that the end was near. "Fought out of Atlantic City, right? Back in the eighties?"

"Yeah, he did. There and Philly, too. But after that last sucker punch he was worthless, gun-shy, couldn't punch himself out of a bag. I tried to bring him back, but he was done. A real shame, too. He coulda reached the top."

The man went on, remembering fights and fighters, glory nights, big purses, sellout crowds, a split decision he swore had robbed his fighter of a shot at the title. He was clueless, lost in his reveries. And Harry, waiting for his moment, nodded, agreed, and exclaimed.

Then at last it seemed over. The man, wearying now, took a long breath and paused.

"How about Tyrone Everett? Do you remember *him?*" Harry asked.

The old man stopped and looked at him, his eyes briefly widening, then raised his hand to his mouth and nodded.

"Everett? Yeah, yeah, I remember him. He was a talented kid, got himself busted or something, didn't he? Went to jail or something like that, right? But he wasn't my fighter, so I never had much truck with him. A lot of those kids like that. They got all kinds of talent, then they get themselves in trouble—women or booze, or they knock over some store or something. They got no patience, they don't want to wait, don't want to put in the work. It's a real shame too, 'cause some of 'em could really climb the ladder . . . "

He went on. Julia, who had waited for a break in the monologue, smiled and said she had to leave; she would wait outside for Harry.

"Next time bring Sarah," the old man called after her as she turned to go.

Harry didn't move.

"So, you gonna bring Sarah to see me, buddy?" the man said. "Or is she too sick to come see her old uncle?"

"Sarah's not coming," Harry said flatly—then spat out his next words.

"Not coming *ever*. You straight on that, '*Uncle Poke*'?"

The man stared back blankly.

"So let's cut the shit, okay? I know who you are, McGuigan. Tyrone Everett was a friend of mine."

"Yeah? You in the fight business or what?"

"Until he got strung up in that jail cell. But I think you know about that."

The man looked around the room nervously, his head swiveling from side to side.

"You talkin' in riddles now," he said. "What you come here for anyway? What you want with me?"

Harry took a step toward the man, then another, until they were close enough to touch. Then he stooped down until their eyes were level, his face an inch away.

"I'm talking about my friend Tyrone. And my friend Sarah. You *murdered* him. You *destroyed* her. That's what I'm talking about."

The man looked back at Harry, plainly frightened now, his eyes blinking wildly.

"You're crazy, I didn't—"

In two short strides Harry was behind the wheelchair, his hands around the man's throat, middle fingers pushing upward into his trachea. The old man gave out a long gasp, then a rasping noise, his fingers clawing frantically at Harry's—"*You're choking me, I can't breathe!*"

"Can't breathe, huh? Must be a real bitch. What was it with *him*?—a sheet? a rope? a belt? What?"

"I didn't do nothin'. Honest, buddy, it wasn't—"

Harry tightened his grip. There was a deep gurgle from the back of the man's throat, then the acrid smell of urine.

"*What was it, asshole?*"

"A rope maybe, I don't remember—*but it wasn't me, I swear!*"

Harry gripped the handles at the back of the chair, dropped it quickly to within inches of the floor, then laid it on its back. The man's head jerked violently. Harry stood, looking down at the pile of squirming, sputtering flesh as it wrestled itself free from the wheelchair onto the linoleum tiles. *"Fuck you, you're crazy,"* it panted up at him.

For another minute, Harry stayed, watching the body writhe and rage as he felt his own anger drain out of him.

"You're nothing," he said. Then he turned and walked from the room, leaving the old man on his back, arms and legs flailing wildly, like an overturned beetle.

Twenty-Five

———

The Tuesday after the Memorial Day holiday, Harry got home from work to find a voicemail from Adele Russo, the lawyer Sarah had hired. She hadn't been able to reach Sarah, she said, but had been given Harry's number as a contact. Had he heard from her?

"I'm sorry about the sad news on the boxer," the message said. "I haven't heard from Sarah in a while. Please have her let me know if she still wants to go ahead with the case, or if there is anything else I can do."

Lennie Wynn was right. The two boxers had been released. But Harry didn't know what to do with the news. He sat the rest of the evening in front of the TV, drinking bourbon and trying not to think. The next morning, he returned the lawyer's call. He needed to talk to someone. Sarah was gone from him, he had no idea to where; Adele Russo was his only connection to her now, and the only person he could trust who wouldn't need a lot of explaining. He had never felt more alone.

He was on hold for what felt like forever. When the lawyer came on, he told her the details of the boxers' release, then of his run-in with

Lennie Wynn and the envelope of cash. He passed on Eel's version of the boxers' story about Tyrone being taken from his cell. "They claim he was murdered," he said.

She listened quietly, then advised him to go to the police. He said he doubted any good would come of that, that a lot of the AC police were as dirty as the mob. He admitted he was scared.

"I don't blame you. But I don't know what to advise you," the lawyer said, with a quiet calm that left him feeling even more alone. "A lot of what you're telling me would be viewed as hearsay, no matter how reliable it might be. But you might consider contacting the attorney general. I know him well, he's as aboveboard as they come. I could make a call to his office in Trenton, lay out the situation, put you in touch with his people there. No names would have to be used, at least initially. Is that something you'd want me to do?"

Harry felt exhausted. He didn't know *what* he wanted, except to be somewhere else. "Maybe at some point," he told her. "Not right now. I think I just need some time."

"I understand," Adele Russo said. "And that's fine. Just have Sarah let me know if there's anything I can do. But it sounds like sooner or later this needs to be in the hands of the police."

The lawyer asked if Harry had a current address or phone number for Sarah. He said he didn't, but promised to let her know when he did.

Then he went into the paper—he could think of nothing else to do—where he spent the rest of the day and most of the week running down a story about a toddler abducted from a Ventnor nursery school.

∗∗∗

In Friday afternoon's mail came a bulky 9-by-12 brown envelope addressed in Sarah's unmistakable schoolgirl hand. Inside were two sheets of lined notebook paper and twenty $100 bills.

Hello you,

Guess what? I saw you at the memorial the other day. I was the guy sitting right behind you on the grass. You were talking to some kid. Pretty good disguise, huh? ☺. Anyway you looked good.

Harry, for all his amazement, couldn't help smiling. He read on:

It's awful what happened to Tyrone. I know how much you liked him. But it isn't going to end there, I promise. Like I told you, I know a lot of really bad stuff, and it's going to come out. I just have to time things right. Like you always said, there's a place and a time, right? ☺.

I'm doing okay. Still hiding out, like you said. That makes it sound like some weird TV spy thing, but that really is about the size of it these days. Anyway I'm okay. You need to go away, Harry. I thought about it, and I think you really do, even if you don't write the story. Please, as soon as you can, before they decide to come after you. And next time it won't be that creep Wynn. I know it'll be hard for you for awhile without your job. That's what the money is for, to get by till you can get settled somewhere. And I know you have to take it cuz you can't find me to pay it back! ☺.

You're a great guy, Harry. We had a lot of fun, right? I know I did. Maybe we'll run into each other again someday if we both make it out of this place. Anyway, please leave soon and take good care of yourself and don't worry about me. I'll be fine.

Sarah

The tears came hard, dribbling onto the pages, smearing the ink. Harry sat numbly, staring at the letter in his hand then holding it to his nose to find a smell, but there was none. The memories of her besieged him: in bed, on the dance floor, in the surf, wretched and shivering in a lukewarm bath . . .

But who was she? As if by some storybook magic she seemed to him now to be all things at once: lover, hooker, mob hostage, girl-child, shape-shifting phantom. Who was she? Where was she? How could she know the things she knew? He put down the letter and gave in to the tears.

It was time to go, she was right about that. But not that day or the next day, not right away. Something held him; he wasn't sure what. Maybe just the certainty that came with leaving: the sure, hard end of something that had once held so much of what had seemed real.

The next day he bought a gun. It was a Smith and Wesson .38, aluminum alloy, two-inch barrel, with a six-round cylinder. Lightweight, only seventeen ounces, it fit without a bulge in any pocket he chose. It cost him $120 and came with twenty-five rounds of ammunition. He hated it—he knew nothing about guns, had never owned one, and the only one he'd ever fired was a single-shot .22 at summer camp when he was twelve. But he carried it everywhere now and kept it next to his bed at night. It made him feel almost safe.

***

A week passed, then a month, then two. Harry threw himself hard into his *Herald* work, reporting stories on card counters, a homeless shelter in the Inlet ("A Bed and Free Meal in the City of Dreams"), a recent wave of Boardwalk muggings, and—lately teamed up with Jack Duffy— the wild, almost daily gyrations of the casino industry.

It was the time of Trump. Of the ten casinos now in the city, two were his already, and another soon would be. He was an endless source of copy. The press coverage was constant, and largely worshipful. There were interviews on "Donahue" and "60 Minutes." He and Ivana were the toast of the city. At *The Herald*, a survey had shown that newsstand sales rose by 10 percent when Trump was on the front page. "Good or bad, savior or shyster, Trump is The Man," Harry wrote in one story. "The city will soar or stumble on his watch."

And already, the stumbling had begun. One casino by then had lost its license, several more were struggling. The industry's profits had dropped 60 percent in the past three years. Traffic into the city—60,000 cars, 1,100 buses daily—seemed unsustainable; street crime was soaring; off the Boardwalk, the commercial district was dying; the airport had no tower, its terminal a jerry-built chain of connected trailers. The resort, less than ten years into its new era, seemed already tarnished, its early gloss a running joke.

July came and went. Harry worked his assignments—none mob-related, the agreement with Alcorn still stood—ran his three miles daily when the weather permitted, and played blackjack at Caesars when he could afford it (though the money from Sarah stayed untouched in his sock drawer). Once in a while, when the prospect of another night alone weighed too heavily, he went after work to The Thirty to drink with Duffy and the crew. Once in the early weeks he went home with a woman, though that felt so empty he resolved to no longer give in to the need.

Every second weekend, as before, he drove north to see Woody—a baseball game, a movie or bowling, sometimes followed by a night at an inn with pool tables and a swimming pool—which brought him pride and pleasure, and felt like the only thing in the world that still mattered.

One Saturday, two months after the memorial for Tyrone, he went to Eel's house on Baltic Avenue to see what was happening with the boy. His mother answered the door, and said that he'd enlisted in the army and was at basic training in Missouri.

He wanted to leave. He had promised himself he would, but could think of nowhere to go, and nowhere else he wanted to be—except back in Connecticut again, reporting on zoning board meetings, watching peewee soccer games, eating dinner every night with his once loved and loving wife and son.

**

On a Tuesday night in mid-August, he found himself sitting at a Caesars blackjack table across from Claire Cellini. She was losing, he could see that—her chip pile was down to two small stacks of reds—though it didn't seem to trouble her. She smiled at Harry from where she sat, and gave a little two-finger wave, which he returned. A few minutes later, she pushed her last five chips in front of her, watched as the dealer pulled a twenty to her own eighteen, looked over at him and motioned toward the mezzanine upstairs.

"Join me?" she said.

Harry had barely begun to play, but was feeling no pull to go on. And the woman's smile warmed him.

"Sure, why not?" he said. "Probably save me some money."

It wasn't yet seven o'clock. The lounge was nearly empty, but the woman walked, like the last time, past the wicker chairs to the bar.

"It's been a while," she said once they'd ordered. "How are you doing? Has our fair city finally worn you down?"

Harry didn't know how to answer. "It's been a long few months," he said.

"I'm sure it has. I read about what happened with your boxer. I'm sorry."

"Thank you," he said, surprised that she had made the connection, or could even remember the name. "Yes, that was a blow. It shouldn't have ended that way."

"But he did burn down that gym, didn't he?"

"He had his reasons. It's a long story, really."

"Yes, they wanted him to throw a fight, as I remember. Isn't that what you said?"

"That's right. Listen, if you don't mind, I'd just as soon not talk about it."

"I understand. So, what should we talk about?"

"Just about anything else," Harry said. "But I've got to be off soon anyway; I have a meeting to go to." This wasn't true, but he could feel his agitation rising.

"How about our friend Vic McGuigan? Wasn't that where we left off last time?"

Harry said nothing, just looked hard at the woman and took a swallow of his drink, which the bartender had just set down in front of him.

"Maybe you don't know the latest on him," the woman said, her voice now taking on a vaguely mocking tone. "Your paper hasn't reported it, this could be your next big story."

"I doubt it," Harry said. "I'm not writing those kinds of stories anymore." He laid a twenty on the bar, ignoring the woman's protest.

"He's *gone*. Disappeared. Kaput. Gone without a trace."

Harry stiffened. "What are you talking about?"

"I mean he's gone. A week ago, maybe longer. He just walked out on all of it—his boxers, his properties, the bimbo he was living with, the whole ball of wax. He owed Sy close to eight grand for some leases he had, but we'll never see that money. The man's just gone. No big surprise, I guess."

"You've lost me," Harry said. He noticed that his hands were starting to shake. He cupped the right one around his glass and put the left in his lap.

"There's nothing else to tell. I heard that somebody turned on him, some boxer maybe, I don't know. They went to the cops with a story. It could have been anything—fight fixing, bribery, extortion.

Or maybe worse. They might have linked him up with what happened to your boxer. I don't know, there's no way of knowing. Anyway, he took off."

"How do you know he took off? How do you know he's not *dead?*"

The woman smiled thinly and shook her head. "He drained his bank accounts. Every dime."

"And how do you know all this?"

Another thin smile. "Word travels."

And in that instant he knew: Of course. She was one of them—she was part of it. Another tiny, polluted drop in this reservoir of poisoned water, each one awaiting its turn as the filthy substance sluices through.

"Wow, you too," he said. It was all he could think to say. He felt emptied. He felt a fool.

She looked at him with what seemed like pity. Then she laid her hand lightly on his forearm and spoke in a gentle tone.

"You went to college, Harry, right? You must have read some of those old Greek myths, Virgil and Plato and all that?" She waited for an answer, but none came, and the woman went on.

"Remember that one about the two lovers? How she was so beautiful, he was handsome and charming, and sang and played beautiful music—then one day she dies and gets sent by the gods to live in the underworld? Remember that? And how he follows to try to get her back? But he doesn't *belong* there, the gods don't want him there. Remember what happens to him?"

Harry just stared at her.

"I told you before, Harry, you should have listened to me then—you're in way over your head. You're a very sweet man, you're nice-looking and smart, a good reporter, and you play a mean game of blackjack. And I *like* you. But this place is the *goddamn underworld,* and you're not cut out for it. The gods don't want you here. I knew it the minute I saw you."

Twenty-Six

———

August 2017

"I could have killed him. I know I wanted to," Harry said.

They were just west of Schenectady, following the Mohawk River east on their drive home. The small, sad farms they'd been passing were giving way to industry: a cannery, a chewing-gum factory, a plant that made mop wringers. You could almost taste the blight.

"I'm glad you didn't," Julia said. She was smiling faintly, half-prone in the reclined passenger's seat. "I can see the headlines—'College Prof Flips Wheelchair, Slays Helpless Geezer in Nursing Home.'"

Harry laughed, but not with much feeling.

"Actually, I'm glad I got to meet him," Julia said. "He's even worse than I imagined. The cruelties you described, they're a lot easier for me to picture now. I'm amazed she's even survived."

"If you can call it survival," Harry said.

"But it *is*, it *is* survival. She came to you, she asked for help, didn't she? She talks to you, she trusts you with those awful secrets. That she could still trust anyone—that's amazing to me."

"Who else could she trust? She doesn't have anyone else."

"You're missing the point, Harry," Julia said, but there was no unkindness in her tone, and when he looked over he saw that her eyes were wet with tears.

"What Sarah's been through, it reminds me of some of the women I've worked with, street women, addicts, women in shelters—only worse. And nearly all of them, they got to where they are the same way. They trusted someone who betrayed them. A father, a husband, a boyfriend, whoever it was. He beat them up, or raped them, or hooked them on drugs, or maybe all of that. And so today they're *broken*— totally broken. They're like zombies, they're dead inside. They can't function, they can't trust anyone, they probably never will.

"But Sarah, she's still fighting, she's still goes on. And she can still *trust*. Given what she's been through, you can't know how amazing that is. I think she might be the bravest person I know."

Harry listened, but felt more anger than sadness.

"This is just so *wrong*," he said. "It's all so, so wrong."

It was all he could manage. What he really felt was more complicated, and he thought now how naive and pious it would sound. Because the truth was that, nearly all his life, and for all the badness he had seen and written about, he had never stopped believing that there was some sort of eventual *rightness* to things—that life unspooled itself in certain ways, and that, even if you couldn't discern it, there was a kind of justice behind it all: People mostly, sooner or later, got what they deserved. He had always believed this. It was the closest he came to a belief in God.

But now, coming off the spectacle of Vic McGuigan's wretchedness, he felt it tested as never before. The images of the twelve-year-old Sarah, raped and brutalized by a father, then pimped out by an uncle, bullied into tears by a sadistic courtroom lawyer, then selling herself for decades on street corners and in barrooms—and now so beaten down at sixty that her only refuge was in pills—were enough to make even the *notion* of justice seem sick.

***

There were two voicemail messages on Harry's phone when they got back, both from Sarah. The first, from the day before, was an apology: "I'm really sorry how I acted yesterday morning. I didn't mean to talk to you that way." The other was from several hours before: "Harry, I got sick. I'm in the hospital in Nashua. Could you maybe bring some clothes from the motel, and my toilet stuff? I'm sorry, I didn't have time to bring them."

An hour later, at around seven o'clock Sunday evening, Julia and Harry sat on either side of Sarah's bed at St. Joseph's. She'd been brought in that morning, after she'd awoken with a headache, dizzy and vomiting, and cramps in her legs and feet so painful she couldn't stand.

She had spent most of that day in and out of labs. The results, the doctor had told Harry, showed her kidney function "deep in the red zone," likely the result of her years of alcohol abuse. An angiogram showed a partial blockage of her main coronary artery, which would require a stent. Even with that, to avoid the "near-certainty" of a stroke or heart attack, the doctor said, "She'll need to stop the drugs she's taking, go on a low-fat, low-sodium diet, and get some regular exercise." Harry doubted she'd do any of it.

"I already quit booze," she said to him. "I hardly ever do benzos anymore, only oxy sometimes. And Xanax. They help me sleep, they keep me calm."

"So you're not going to quit? You're not going to even try?"

"Maybe I'll try. Would you like that? Would that make you happy?"

Harry was angry. And afraid. He had no plan, no real roadmap from the doctors on what to expect, and no faith in Sarah's own efforts. He feared leaning too hard on Julia. His savings had dwindled badly, along with his hope. Always before he had looked forward to fall, the beginning of things at the college. This year he felt only dread.

They brought her some supper from a take-out place nearby: chicken breast, mashed potatoes, broccoli, and mandarin oranges, most of which she left on her plate. She was rail-thin, her eyes red-rimmed and her skin so pale it looked almost translucent. But her spirits seemed to be holding up.

She apologized again to Harry for her angry words of Friday morning, while explaining to Julia that she'd been "a real nutcase. I'm glad you weren't around to see it." Then she said she had some "bad news"—she'd been laid off at Costco. Too many missed days, she said. Then she began to cry.

Harry reached across and took her hand. "I might be able to find you something at the college, maybe some clerical work, something part-time," he said. "I've been thinking of that anyway."

Sarah nodded, smiled weakly, and withdrew her hand. Harry moved her dishes to a small shelf by the window, and was about to suggest that they should leave and let her sleep when Sarah turned abruptly to Julia, who had been quiet.

"Did he tell you about the other night?"

No one spoke. Sarah waited, then began turning her head jerkily from one of them to the other. Finally Julia answered.

"About your father, you mean?"

"Yes, about what I told him. About what I did."

"Yes, Harry told me. That must have been horrible for you. But you were very young, Sarah, you were almost a child. I don't think you should blame yourself for anything that happened."

Her voice was soft and very even. Harry opened his mouth to speak but she went on.

"We took a road trip this weekend. To your old town, to Ripton—it isn't that far away. We saw where you used to live with your father. I hope you don't mind."

Sarah's hands went to her mouth. She began swiveling her head again, to Harry, then back to Julia, then to Harry again.

"I don't mind," she said. But the house is gone. It burned down."

"We saw that."

"And then you left, you just drove home?"

Julia looked quickly at Harry, who started to look away. But Sarah had caught it.

"No, you didn't. You went somewhere else. Please tell me where you went."

"After your father died, you went to live with your uncle, right?"

Sarah nodded.

"And do you know where he is now?"

Sarah shook her head slowly. "In jail maybe?"

"He was in jail for a while"—it was Harry who spoke now. "But he's been out for a long time. He lives in Utica now, in a nursing home. We went to see him there."

Sarah said nothing. Julia had her phone in her hand now, scrolling. She found what she was looking for, then handed it to Sarah. "I took a couple of pictures. I thought you might want to see."

She passed the phone to Sarah. Two photos she'd taken earlier in the nursing home: Vic McGuigan in his wheelchair, eyes wide and mouth tightly shut, arms raised from the elbows, palms up, as if to express confusion or indifference. Both showed wretchedness.

For a long time, Sarah just stared—holding the phone in both hands, her lips pursed, her eyes fixed and narrowed, seeming to try to devour every detail, or stare it into oblivion.

"Where is he?" she said finally.

"Like Harry said, in a nursing home," Julia said. "He can't leave, he can't go anywhere, he has no visitors. He couldn't be more harmless."

"Did he ask about me?"

"Yes. He talked about you quite a lot . . . Would you like to see him? There's no need for you to, but we could take you there if you want."

Sarah didn't answer. She hadn't stopped staring. It seemed to Harry that she might be about to scream or cry, or break completely. A minute went by, frozen.

"He scared me *so much*," she said then, numbly, still staring at the picture.

"I know he did," Harry said. He had pulled his chair closer to her bed. "He did awful things to you. But he doesn't have to scare you anymore."

"*You know*, don't you?" Sarah said, her voice now a quaver. "You know what he did."

"Yes, we do. We know what he did. And we know *who he is*." Harry hadn't planned to say this, but wasn't sorry he had. He looked across at Julia, who seemed to smile, then looked away.

"I'm *glad* you know," Sarah said then. "I didn't want you to know, but now I'm glad you do. That's crazy, isn't it?" She was smiling crookedly.

"Not crazy at all," Julia said. "You were holding in a lot of things. You don't have to do that anymore."

Watching Sarah's strange, half-guilty smile and listening now to Julia's reassurances, Harry was caught suddenly in another whirl of memory and emotion: Sarah's arms flung in the air on the Ferris wheel at Six Flags, at the Stone Harbor beach in her green-and-yellow two-piece. For much of the past weeks he had felt removed from his love for her, conscious only of her misery and need for help. The power of it now was almost hypnotic. He wanted to enfold her.

They talked for another hour, until the nurse came in and said it was time to go. Sarah told them of things Harry knew only sketchily: of riding Greyhounds between cities to chase the latest convention; the loneliness, betrayals, indignities and small kindnesses; the sickness and early death of her mother, whom she'd rarely mentioned before. She spoke of crimes and disappearances Vic McGuigan had spoken of or forced her to witness, lives ruined and bodies disposed of. Some of these, she said, she had testified to on a court-monitored recording; it was part of what had sent her uncle to prison, where (as Harry would learn later) he had spent close to fifteen years. Of Tyrone, she said only that she had heard his death mentioned several times—usually as part of "one of their sick talks"—but that she was pretty sure they were behind it.

Toward the end, at Julia's prodding, she talked about her daughter, Maryanne.

"She's *his*. But he never knew her, he never even saw her. I was pregnant that last time I saw you back then"—this addressed to Harry now—"in that place on the Boardwalk where we met. But I wasn't sure yet, and I wouldn't have told you anyway. She was born in Philly that next year. I couldn't keep her, my life was such a mess. But I always meant to go back and try to find her . . .

"But then she found *me*, when she was sixteen, I think. That was when I told her the story about the race-car driver being her daddy—he was *real*. I knew him. His name was Matteo Ricci, and he was killed racing on a track in Florida. I liked him, even though I only saw him a few times. He gave me a silver charm—Saint Sebastian, the saint of good luck for race drivers, he said. He had one just like it, even though it didn't protect *him*, I guess. I gave mine to Maryanne. She still has it, on a necklace, I think. She has his picture too, from a magazine story after he died. She keeps it in this little wood frame.

"I've always thought I should tell her the truth, so she could know who her real daddy was. But now I don't know if I will."

Through most of this, Sarah remained calm, even laughing at herself once. Then, gradually toward the end, she grew more morose, her voice shriller. She asked Harry for help maneuvering her into the wheelchair at the foot of the bed. He wheeled her to the bathroom, where she remained for several minutes. By the time she returned, she was as calm as before. She lay back, closed her eyes and sighed deeply, then opened them again and reached for Harry's hand.

"I don't need to see him," she said quietly, looking up at him. "I don't want to see him ever again."

"That's fine, Sarah," Harry said. "And he doesn't have to scare you anymore. Where he is now, the way he is, I promise you he can't hurt anyone."

Sarah nodded weakly. "I'm so tired," she said. "I'm just so tired."

"We'll leave you to rest," Julia said, and she and Harry got up to leave. When Harry reached down to hug her, she took ahold of his shirt and pulled him close, until his ear was an inch from her mouth. Julia looked away.

"*I'm done, Harry,*" she whispered, so quietly he could barely make out the words.

* * *

They discharged her two days later. Harry drove her to his place, where she slept all afternoon. Julia arrived later with three live lobsters packed in seaweed—Sarah's birthday had passed two days before; she had said once that lobster was her favorite meal.

They ate dinner on the deck. It was a warm, clear, late-August evening, capped with cake and non-alcoholic champagne. As the sun dropped lower, the river glinted a pale pink. Sarah seemed to be enjoying herself. She put on the funny paper hat Julia had brought, beamed like a child to their duet of "Happy Birthday," and made a big show of blowing out the candles.

They talked of small things: the new Spider-Man movie, country music, the beauty of sunsets over the Pacific, which Sarah said she remembered from her time in LA. She said she hoped Julia's daughter and hers might meet one day. She asked Harry to tell her about the books they read in his classes; she had read *A Farewell to Arms* in her only semester at college, and thought it was "the saddest, most beautiful story I ever heard." Harry asked what other books she liked; she answered that he wouldn't know of most of them—"just trashy love stories," she said, and laughed self-consciously.

By then it was past eleven. Julia said goodnight, held Sarah in a long hug—"Happy birthday, my brave new friend. I'm so glad you're here with us"—and went upstairs to bed.

"You're a lucky man," Sarah said, when they were alone. "I hope you know how lucky you are."

"I do," Harry said. "I think of it every day."

The two of them sat quietly, listening to the river behind them. Sarah finished the last of the champagne; Harry went inside, poured himself a long shot of bourbon and brought it outside in a Styrofoam birthday cup.

"So have you had a good birthday? Sixty-one, right? Or sixty-two?"

"One, I think," said Sarah. "I'm not exactly sure. Anyway, I'm *old*."

"You're younger than I am," Harry answered.

"No, I'm not. I'm *way* older," she said.

Harry didn't answer, fearing where this exchange could drift. He felt a new heaviness between them now, as though the air had grown thicker with Julia's departure. They talked a few minutes more, about not much of anything, before he said he was tired and ready for bed.

"Couldn't we sit a little while longer?" Sarah asked quietly. "This is nice, just sitting and hearing the river, listening to the river. It's so peaceful."

Harry said he didn't mind, though he feared what might be coming. He would have liked another drink, but got them both a ginger ale instead. They were sitting a foot apart, in adjoining wicker chairs.

There was a crescent moon. The river was invisible now; only the inside lamps lit the deck. Sarah looked away, sighed, then looked at Harry.

"I'm ready to go," she said softly. Harry said nothing.

"Do you know what I'm saying?"

"I think I do, yes."

"I need you to understand."

"I do understand," he said. "You've been through a lot. You're tired, you're drained emotionally. You can't trust your thinking right now."

Sarah's voice cracked, then grew louder.

"*No.* That's not it. I can't do it anymore. I'm sick. And there are too many lies."

"What lies? What do you mean?"

"You know, all the lies I keep telling. I've been lying my whole life— about my name, who I am, who I was, the lie to Maryanne about Matteo. I've been thinking all along I had to tell her the truth. I couldn't stop thinking that, it was driving me crazy. So then I'd take more pills."

"You want her to know the truth?"

"*No.* She can't know who he is, not that creep in the wheelchair"— and here Sarah let out a small laugh. "He used to scare me *so much.* I'd be seeing him in my dreams, almost every night. I was sure he was gonna come after me. I know it sounds crazy, but I was."

There was a long silence, nothing but river sounds and the distant call of a night bird.

"I've had a hard life, Harry."

"Yes, you have. Way harder than you deserved."

"No, I deserved it. But the hardest part has been just keeping on."

Harry reached over and took her hand.

"I'm tired. I've had enough."

Harry nodded. He said he understood.

"I'm glad," she said. "I need you to." And she leaned over and kissed him lightly on the lips.

Then she began to ramble: Maryanne as an infant and baby girl, her shame at having to give her up, the guilt she was feeling now in wanting to leave her again—"But I've been no kind of mother to her, always too broke or too trashed to make it right." And finally of Harry and Atlantic City: afternoons at the beach, the jade elephant necklace he'd given her, which she confessed she'd later had to pawn.

"You *knew* me. You *always* knew me. You're the only one who ever did. The only one who ever even tried."

"That can't be true," Harry said.

"Well, maybe Julia. But she comes with you, it's kind of a two-for-one thing."

Harry tried to laugh. "You're very worth knowing," he said.

She went on and on. She seemed almost to be enjoying herself now. Then, in the middle of it all, she stopped abruptly and took a long breath.

"I need you to help me," she said.

"Help you with what?"

"To do it. I told you, I'm done."

Harry didn't know he'd stopped breathing until he started again.

"What are you talking about?"

"I'm sick, Harry. I feel like crap all the time, every day. I'll probably die soon anyway unless I stop the pills, and you know I'll never do that. I'm ready to go. But I need you to help me."

"This is crazy, Sarah. Let's not even talk about it."

"Please. You want me around like *this*, in and out of detox, getting sicker and sicker, with you writing checks the whole time? For what?"

"Please, Sarah, don't even think about the money. That's not—"

"Listen to me, *please*. I know what I want to do."

"Okay, tell me."

"I want to drown. In the river."

Harry gathered himself, trying to match the soberness he was hearing. "You could do that without me. If that's what you really want."

"No, I can't, I'm way too much of a chicken. I'd probably just mess it up and wind up in the hospital again."

"What do you want me to do, *hold you under?*"

"You won't have to. I'll take a bunch of pills to start with, so I'll be pretty wrecked. And you know I can't swim anyway. You'll be there just in case."

"In case of what?"

"In case I chicken out." It was as though she was talking about an amusement-park ride.

"It sounds like you've been planning this for a while."

"I have. I told you. Please help me do it . . . I don't want to be alone."

"I can't talk about this anymore, Sarah. It's too much. It's like you're asking me to commit murder."

"No. It'll be like mercy, that's all, like what you'd do for a dog or a cat. And no one will think anything. Everybody knows I'm an addict. I'll just be an old addict who got high and fell in the river and drowned."

Harry kept saying he wouldn't talk about it, but they talked about it anyway, as the night turned cooler and the moon rose in the sky behind them. They were still talking well past midnight, when Harry went inside and brought out a bag of Doritos and bottled water, and they ate and talked some more. Sarah wanted to die, and she wanted him to help her. She asked over and over, the same plea sometimes in different words: that she was dying anyway, it would be easier to go quickly; that she was tired of living and wanted to go—she always used that same word, 'go'—that she was an addict and wouldn't quit till it killed her, and would he really want that? And that she didn't want to be alone.

"I want you to be the last person I see," she said.

He saw how doomed she was. He had always seen that. A part of him wanted to say yes, but he couldn't let himself. He tried to picture it: watching her go under, then fight to come up, to breathe, to live—as he knew she would—then pushing her back down. But he couldn't imagine any of it. And he couldn't imagine the world without her.

"I can't do it," he said. "You're asking me to do something I can't do. Please, Sarah, don't ask me to do this."

But she wouldn't let it go. And sometimes, if you try long and hard enough, you can imagine almost anything. The unthinkable becomes thinkable: a divorce, a terminal illness, a suicide. Even murder—or *assisted suicide*, which was what both of them were calling it to themselves by the end.

Twenty-Seven

———

It was just past three o'clock on a Friday afternoon—August 17, 1987—when Harry, his car packed and his final story filed, drove for the last time through the tollbooth at the northbound entrance to the Garden State. The city was filling like a sand glass. At the southbound tolls coming the other way, the traffic had started to clog. By five o'clock, he knew, the cars would be backed up half a mile. By seven the expressway into the city would be choked in fumes and the casino garages would be turning away drivers. By eight the madness would have moved indoors. ("Modulated chaos," Harry had written of it once in an early column: "Less in winter, more in summer, worst over holiday weekends . . .The dance of the slot creatures." But he had no such thoughts today.)

The wind was up and gusting, but it was a warm wind and the sun was out for the first time in a week. Bits of cellophane and brown paper skittered across the northbound lanes, which were as flat and empty as a tarmac. To the west and east, flat-roofed discount motels shared space with mocha-colored condos and "Family Style" restaurants. It could as easily have been Nebraska.

It was true what Claire Cellini had said: Vic McGuigan had disappeared, wanted by the state for solicitation, racketeering and several lesser crimes. ("He had his dirty fingers in every racket in town," she had said of him. "A greedy son of a bitch is what he was.") Toby Ward and Ruben Florio were awaiting trial. The investigation into Tyrone's death had been reopened. And while there were no witnesses or complainants named in the records Harry had seen, there was a reference to a "secondary source" and another to "relevant tape-recorded testimony." More would come out later, but for now this was all there was to know. Sarah, it seemed, had made good on her promise.

She was gone. Or at least unfindable. That much was sure. There was no doubt someone somewhere, some prosecutor or DA, who would know who and where she was, but Harry had tried every door he knew—Adele Russo, Jack Duffy, the attorney general's office, a private detective he'd once used as a source—and none of them had opened even a crack.

He knew already that, however long his life, he would remember these years as its darkest. But also as its most full-hearted, its most real. The sureness of this over the past several days had filled him with such almost unbearable sadness that now, headed north away from it all, he felt next to nothing.

The reasons were gone, but the rhythms remained in place: It was a summer Friday and he was driving north toward his son. That was all that seemed sure, or worth caring for.

Twenty-Eight

————

October 2017

The stillwater just downriver from Harry's home, three miles south of where the Shawsheen joins the Merrimack, is roughly sixty feet from bank to bank, between three and seven feet deep—deepest toward the middle—rocky-bottomed and thickly lined with trees. It was raining lightly and nearly moonless when Harry half-carried Sarah down its west bank, scrabbling across roots and rocky outgrowth by the light of his headlamp. Sarah wore the same blue sweatshirt she'd arrived in four months before, jeans, sneakers and a backward Red Sox cap. Harry was in shorts and a T-shirt. She was stumbling badly. He was crying. Neither one was talking. It was a Thursday morning, October 12, 2017, a little past three a.m.

It had been more than a month since they'd first talked about it, a week since he had agreed to Sarah's plea. Twice since then they'd set a date. Both times he'd backed out. But now it was time, and his conditions were met: a weeknight, overcast, no classes scheduled that morning. He had picked her up, as arranged, at the Ebb Tide at one a.m. and driven to his house, where he drank two more bourbons on top of the ones he'd had, and Sarah had a brandy on top of her oxy.

She was slurring her words and was sick in the bathroom, but seemed as untroubled as though she'd just arrived for dinner.

There was no more need for words. They had thought and talked it into smallness, almost to nothingness. Harry marveled that he could have taught classes all the day before, met with students, laughed and made jokes with a colleague in the afternoon, knowing where he was to be in twelve hours. *Only a monster could be that unfeeling*, he thought.

Yet now, in the last hour, he was falling apart. On the deck with Sarah just minutes before, he had tried a final time to dissuade her. She was reacting to old demons, he said; Maryanne would feel abandoned; drowning could be a painful way to go.

Sarah was unfazed.

"We made a deal—please don't mess this up for me," she said.

In the end she had extended her hand, he had taken it, and they had walked off the deck together.

And now they were in the water, just past their ankles, a yard or so off the bank. It felt colder to Harry than he'd expected. Sarah was staggering as she moved, her dulled senses no match for the rocky bottom. Harry had his arm around her waist; she lurched against him with every step.

"It's going to get deeper now," he said. "I've got you." He was sobbing quietly; the words were hard to get out.

"I know," Sarah said. "I'm scared, Harry."

"We can turn back anytime," he said.

"*No! Please no!* Don't let me chicken out."

They took two more steps toward the middle. The river was past Harry's knees now, almost to Sarah's waist.

"Hold me for a minute, please?" she said.

He drew her against him and they stood, pressed together, his arms around her waist and shoulders, his face buried in her hair. He could feel her trembling against him.

"What'll happen afterward?" she asked then. "In the river, to my body?"

"The current will take you," Harry said. "You'll wash up somewhere, probably close by. Someone will find you."

They stood silently together for another half-minute. Then Sarah pulled her head back and looked up at him.

"Goodbye, Harry . . . Please, say goodbye."

"Goodbye, Sarah," Harry said between sobs.

"Think of me sometimes, okay?" she said. And with that she pulled away from him suddenly and staggered toward the middle. Within seconds she was over her head and thrashing, grabbing at rocks. Harry went after her, reached her, and took hold of her waist. He was treading water now, the bottom just below his feet.

"This is crazy!" he cried. "Please, Sarah!"

"Let me go!" she sputtered and pulled free of him again. Again he followed. She was choking down water now, flailing, grabbing for his head. He felt the headlamp go.

For a second they went under together, Sarah writhing madly. He lost his hold on her; when he came up there was only blackness. He could hear her near him, still thrashing. His hand found her shoulder. "Do it!" she gasped, and he moved his hand to her head and pushed her under, holding her there. For a little while she wrestled, her arms grabbing at him, her feet kicking out at his legs. Soon, sooner than he expected—he couldn't have said how long—the wrestling became a dull squirm, then just a head jerk, then nothing. Harry loosened his hold and felt her start to drift away. He reached out to touch her in the blackness, but she was already gone.

Twenty-Nine

———

November 2017

The bar at Trump Plaza is empty but for the two of them. There is a buzz of people from the casino floor but no one in sight. Sarah is in that same black satin dress, low-cut and sleeveless with spaghetti straps, her hair in waves to her shoulders. She has never looked so beautiful. She is sitting next to him, her hand on his arm, and he is rapt, intoxicated by her. Then, unexpectedly, she turns her head away and he follows her look, to see that the oval space behind the bar is now a massive fishbowl, with gleaming coral and water to the ceiling, and then Sarah is there too, breaststroking gorgeously, her hair billowed behind her, like a nymph or a mermaid, her face alight with joy. Harry moves to join her, but he is rooted to his barstool, paralyzed, gaping but unable to rise. He reaches out, but it is too far, and she turns and swims away.*

He woke up sobbing, alone in his bed. The realness of it assailed him—he could still feel her in the room, the sense of her everywhere. She was there with him. She was real.

It was a Saturday morning, three weeks since they had found her body washed up on the far shore a quarter-mile downstream, half-covered in duckweed. The police had come and gone; an autopsy report listed the death as a drowning, with "opioid intoxication" a contributing cause. Harry had gone through the days numbly, his focus narrowed to essentials. He had called Maryanne—or Mare, as he had learned she preferred to be called—who arrived on a bus from Philadelphia, quietly leveled by the news. They had gone together to the Ebb Tide to clear out Sarah's belongings and pay the final bill, then to the crematorium, where they had watched the heavy iron door open and close and Sarah disappear for the final time behind it. They both had signed some papers. There would be a small marker in the local cemetery, which Harry would pay for.

"I never really got to know her," Mare had said to him, the morning after she arrived. "She was so messed up by the time we met up—I just never got to know who she was."

"She was very sick. And very troubled," Harry said. "But a beautiful person. And she loved life—she embraced it right till the end. I've never known anyone like her."

"Was she a prostitute?"

This came out of nowhere, the first question of many. It stunned Harry, who was careful with his answers from then on.

"You don't know a lot about her, I guess?"

"Not a lot, no. She didn't share much."

"Yes, she was. For a while. She had no real choice."

"Is that how you met her?"

"She was a source for a story I was writing. I was a reporter then. In Atlantic City."

"Were you in love with her?"

"Yes."

"That's what she said. But I wasn't sure if I believed her. She used to lie a lot."

Harry didn't know what to make of this young woman. She seemed to him terribly earnest, but also fragile, with an almost child-like innocence. In some ways, she reminded him of her mother: guileless, credulous, quietly passionate, with some of the same sense of wounded-ness about her. But with none of Sarah's toughness, or none that he could see. He was afraid he might say too much.

"Your mother was a complicated person, Mare. Sometimes she hid things. She had her reasons for that."

They were sitting at the time in a booth at a local diner, the same one Sarah and Harry had sat in several weeks before. When Harry told this to Mare, she asked if she was sitting on the same side her mother had. He said that she was.

"*Wow*," she said, but very softly, with a delighted smile. Then she settled herself back further into the booth and placed her arm along the length of the backrest.

"I wish she was here now. We could share this breakfast. We did that sometimes, when we didn't have enough for two." With this, she blinked twice, hard, and Harry saw that she was trying not to cry.

***

Julia knew it all by then. Harry had waited till they'd found the body, then called her. She came right away. That same evening, less than forty-eight hours after he had led Sarah by the hand down to the river-bank, he told her how it had happened.

She didn't say a word through the telling. Then, from her chair on the deck next to his, with the sun just gone behind them, she took his hand. "*Oh, Harry*," she whispered, then drew him into her shoulder and gently kissed the top of his head. He looked in her eyes and saw that there was no blame there, only sorrow. He couldn't have needed that more, or been more grateful.

Two weeks later came the dream—followed by an explosion of grief like nothing he had ever known. Memories pummeled him: Sarah in her silly paper hat blowing out her birthday candles, in her backward Red Sox cap pulling away from him in the water ("Think of me sometimes, okay?"). He remembered things he hadn't thought of in years: the living room of her old Ventnor apartment, the smell of her sweat after dancing, the way she squeezed her eyes shut when she came. A parade of images—sounds, smells, pictures—strobed across his mind, one almost on top of another. The only sense was of chaos: an image of Sarah choking down water would be followed by one of his mother lying dead—which he had seen briefly, but erased—then one of Sarah on the beach or in bed. The feeling of loss, and catastrophe, somehow conflated them all.

For two hours he lay there in his bed, sobbing, finally just staring at the wall. He felt emptied out—as though he had been turned upside-down and all his contents, his thoughts and feelings, the certainties he tried to live by, had spilled out of him until he was hollow, until there was nothing left.

She was still there with him at the end. Still as vital, still as deeply mourned.

But no longer real. He saw this now, clearly, for the first time, with a longing so deep he felt the burn of bile in his throat: She had never been real. He had never known her. Who could know such a person? Who could comprehend a life in such pain? She had invented herself, all of her selves. What else could she have done? But he had loved her nonetheless. He always would.

Epilogue

———

Memorial Day 2018

It is the last day of the long weekend, cool and nearly cloudless with a breeze off the river. At the far edge of the deck, Harry is tending a grill. "Burgers or kielbasa?" he calls out, but no one answers. "Just cook some of each and leave it up to them," Julia tells him from nearby, where she is ladling out scoops of potato salad into a ceramic bowl. Behind them on the deck, Mare is deep in conversation with Sameer, a young student from the college, whom Harry has invited over to join them. Woody, with his new wife, Lynn—it is his second marriage—is inside, playing Pick Up Sticks on the living room floor with his five-year-old son. Julia's daughter, Faith, who just split from a long-time boyfriend, is on the couch, reading a *National Geographic* story about zebras.

The holiday is bittersweet. It will be Harry's last in the house. Eight weeks ago, lying together in his bed on a late-winter morning, Julia had asked him: "So where do you see us going?" It was unexpected. They had just made love; he was looking out at the snow bending the bough of a birch tree outside the window. For long seconds his mind stopped. Then the old fear lifted, and he answered. "I see us together," he said.

The house has been sold. Harry has given notice at the college; by summer's end, he will move with Julia into a Dutch Colonial they've bought just south of Boston. For the next year, he'll teach journalism as an adjunct at UMass, where Julia also teaches. What will come after that, he doesn't know.

He will miss his students. And his colleagues, and the comfortable ease of New Boston. And it's been a hard decision to forfeit tenure. But the future seems real now. And it would feel too ghostly to stay.

The afternoon has moved on. Sameer departed first, effusive in his thanks for the meal and company. Woody and his family left next, for home—New Haven, a two-hour drive south—while Julia and Faith, with the dishes stacked now in the kitchen, have gone for a walk, where Faith will pour out her heart to her mother about her lost love. Harry has promised to clean up.

***

It has grown cooler. Harry and Mare have moved indoors to the living room, where they sit now at opposite ends of the couch. Harry has put on a sweater and brought out a woolen throw for Mare. She is here often lately. In the seven months since she lost her mother, she's come north at least once every month—and seems more lost each time. On her last visit, she made Harry take her to the spot where Sarah's body washed up, then sat on the rocks there, alone, for most of an afternoon.

"I feel like, all those years I didn't have a mother, then I found her and now I've lost her again," she had said to Julia the month before.

The veterinarian job in Philadelphia has ended—layoffs, a firing, it's impossible to know from the little she's said. Julia has found her a spot as a circulation assistant at the library at UMass. The pay is meager, but it will keep her close, which seems to matter more to her than anything.

"I can't believe there are no pictures of her," she says to Harry now, not for the first time. "There must be one around somewhere, don't you think?"

Harry thinks of the many old booking photos that must be lying around in local police files, then erases the thought from his mind.

"I kind of doubt it, Mare. I know I didn't take any—she never let me. And I don't know who else would have."

"God, that just seems so wrong. I mean, I have a picture of my dad and I never even *met* him—he died in that crash before I was born. But nothing of her. It's like she *never existed*."

"I know what you mean," Harry says. "I think sometimes she may have felt that way herself."

Mare nods, then shakes her head. "You knew her better than anyone, I guess."

"That might be true."

"What was she like? I mean before this, when you first knew her?"

So for the next hour, Harry tells her stories: of beach days, dancing at Memories—"This old DJ, he called her 'the Dancing Queen'"—his moped crash in Sea Isle City, Sarah's opening strike in her first attempt at bowling—"She shrieked like a little kid at that"—her love of coffee ice cream and sappy movies.

"She was like a child in a lot of ways," Harry says. "You remind me of her a little."

"I guess that's good," Mare says.

"It's *very* good. Sometimes I think we should all be a little more like children."

Then he tells her about the dream.

"She was a mermaid. She had fins; she could swim like a fish—anywhere she wanted, wherever she wanted to go. And she was beautiful, and so happy. Her face was full of joy. I love thinking of her that way."

"Kind of like heaven," Mare says, "like swimming in heaven."

"Yes, exactly like that," Harry says, "like swimming in heaven."

And as he says it, he feels his heart go out to this person he barely knows: this plain, guileless, now motherless child who's spent half her life in foster homes, who seems so terribly lost. She will never be her mother—but she is her child. And she deserves a better fate. And he will do what he can.

"I have an idea," he says now. "How about we all go bowling tomorrow?"

Mare gives a puzzled look, then the small, shy smile he is coming to know.

"That'd be fun," she says. "But I'm not a very good bowler."

"You'll be great, I promise," Harry says. "Your mother was a natural."

About the Author

――――

*G*eoffrey Douglas is the author of five nonfiction books, all widely reviewed. One of them, The Game of Their Lives, was adapted for a 2005 movie of the same name. He has also worked as a reporter, columnist, editor and publisher, and is the author of many magazine pieces. For several years through the 1980s, he was editor of an investigative weekly in Atlantic City, an experience that provided much of the material for Love in a Dark Place, his first work of fiction. He lives today in New Hampshire.

Author's Note

———

My first visit to Atlantic City was in the late fall of 1977. The statewide referendum to allow casinos there—billed as a "noble experiment" to rescue the dying resort from the torpor of crime and poverty it had been sinking into for decades —had passed a year before. Resorts International, the nation's first casino east of Nevada, would open six months later, to be followed by nine more within the next five years. Between them in those years, they would have 12,000 hotel rooms, 350,000 square feet of gambling space and over $5 billion in revenues. No American city in a century had experienced such an overnight rebirth.

Like Harry, my protagonist in this book, I was a young reporter then—on a magazine assignment to cover the story, which was fast becoming national news. Also like Harry, I was captivated by it: fascinated on every level by what seemed to me a kind of morality play. I knew by then of the mounting mob war for control of the city's rackets; I knew of the desperation of poor Blacks in the North Inlet neighborhood, suddenly in danger of losing their homes; I had followed the resort's long history of corruption, which showed no signs of abating. To me, the coming of casinos, with its tens of millions of dollars already flooding the area, felt like a bomb about to drop.

There is one very particular scene I remember from that first visit, which I watched being repeated several times in the following days and weeks. I don't know if it would strike me the same way today—I was barely out of my twenties at the time, an easy mark for lazy metaphors. But it has been more than forty years now, and the memory remains just as redolent.

In the entry hall of the old Merrill Lynch office in downtown Atlantic City, at any hour of any weekday afternoon, they would be the first sight that greeted you: the same twenty or thirty old men, pensioners mostly, in baseball caps, golf shirts or baggy cardigans, in rows of metal folding chairs, their eyes locked on the wall-mounted video monitor, wildly huzzahing, hand-clapping, occasionally groaning, at every eighth-point tick in the price of Resorts International stock— whose value, over the two years following the referendum, would rise from 67 cents to 70 dollars a share.

A few of the men would grow very rich. One I knew parlayed a $60,000 profit into the down payment on a falling-down three-story townhouse he later sold to Harrah's for $4.5 million. Another, I would learn years later, parlayed his profits —nearly his entire life savings at the time—into the shares of another casino, still on the drawing board. The project failed, and the man took his life.

But whatever their outcomes, those men I watched in that broker-age hallway all those years ago were a small mirror of the men and woman, rich and poor, all over the city and region. Atlantic City, in the months and years that followed that November '76 vote, was almost insane with dreams: of stock hits, lands buys, dealer schools, parking lots, restaurant start-ups, liquor stores, pawnshops—everybody had a plan and a dream. The plans would mostly stall and the dreams would erode, gradually, sadly, over the next several years, as the crime and corruption and politicians' arrests mounted like maggots on a corpse. But for that year and the two or three that followed, they remained as fervent and unsullied as religion.

Almost no one was immune to them. I wasn't. My dream, though, was of *stories*: monster stories with human faces that would engage and appall our sense of justice, celebrate the underdog and bring retribution to the wrongdoer. I had been weaned on Watergate, and dreams of Pulitzers. I was a young fool with noble intentions.

And so, in the late summer of 1978, three months after Resorts had opened its doors to the biggest crowd ever seen at a U.S. resort, I paid $22,500 for the name and meager receivables of a defunct weekly paper that had lasted three months. I renamed it *The Sun*—"Your Paper in a Changing Time." Its circulation peaked at 45,000; its target reader was the South Jersey resident who—I felt very sure—was being poorly served by the sleepy local daily and would respond to a fresh perspective in a turbulent time.

"There may be [nowhere] on this continent where the change is as rapid or as wholesale . . . where as many lives are in flux, as many new faces are arriving or as many dollars being spent," I wrote that September in a front-page editorial in the paper's inaugural issue. "We will pinpoint that change, freeze it, for the moment, in a column of copy or a page of photos, give meaning to what we all are living through . . .

To be sure, the stories came, sometimes almost nonstop. Casinos cut deals with senators to sidestep building codes, mayors rigged bids for contractors in exchange for cash (then were indicted or went to jail, just as regularly); the bodies of mob victims turned up in car trunks at the rate of nearly two a month. In the North Inlet, where land values were suddenly doubling every six months, blocks of tenements burned to the ground in "fires of undetermined origin"—for a time, the city's main answer to urban redevelopment. Zoning codes were ignored or loopholed, casino permits were bought with votes or cash. For at least the first three or four years, it was a free-for-all of unbridled greed.

But the stories alone were never enough. The paper, after an eight-year struggle to stay afloat, was bought for the price of its IRS debt by a media firm that saw its future as a tabloid for beach reading—and I departed for Vermont, my small inheritance long gone, to write a novel I would never manage to sell. The early dreams were mostly dead by then.

For the longest time, all this felt too personal to try to tell—those were difficult years, in more ways than would be useful to describe. But a lot of time has passed. And the stories keep coming back to me—and seem to have to have more than ever to say.

***

Harry is the main filter through whom I've told l this story, and he carries with him much of my young-idealist self. But there is also a second principal: Sarah, a $1,000-a-night escort shackled to the mob by an unspeakable secret and her own tragic innocence. For her, there is no analog in my own life. She is fictional—but as real to me as almost anyone I know. Atlantic City in those days was a trolling ground for Sarahs (and perhaps still is): beautiful, misfitted wanderers, each with their own small or large dreams, who are somehow exploited or betrayed by those who see a use for them.

Harry's love for her is not meant to be explicable, any more than my own. She is a doomed innocent who casts a very bright light. Her story should speak for itself.

***

There are several people to whom I owe thanks. The first is Andra Miller, a freelance editor with a long history of successes, who took on this book in its earliest form and guided it through its several incarnations, always with wisdom, patience and the sure instincts of the consummate pro that she is. This would be a far lesser book had we not met.

The next is the team at the Greenleaf Book Group, especially Sally Garland and Benito Salazar (and Mimi Bark, who designed exactly the cover I'd imagined), who shepherded the book through its pre-publication stages with all the class, good judgement and professionalism any author could ask.

And finally my wife, Landon, about whom no words could deliver the true weight due. From first to last, she took on this project almost as her own—from wall charts and day-long reads to the endless hours of my repetitive chatter. She never stopped listening or believing. Without her faith, understanding and frequent marvelous wisdom, this book might never have been started, much less finished. In the end, "Thank you, Love" is all there is to say.